DANGEROUS
BOY

DANGEROUS
BOY

MANDY HUBBARD

An Imprint of Penguin Group (USA) Inc.

Dangerous Boy

RAZORBILL

Published by the Penguin Group
Penguin Young Readers Group
345 Hudson Street, New York, New York 10014, U.S.A.
Penguin Group (USA) Inc., 375 Hudson Street, New York, New York 10014, U.S.A.
Penguin Group (Canada), 90 Eglinton Avenue East, Suite 700, Toronto, Ontario, Canada
M4P 2Y3 (a division of Pearson Penguin Canada Inc.)
Penguin Books Ltd, 80 Strand, London WC2R 0RL, England
Penguin Ireland, 25 St Stephen's Green, Dublin 2, Ireland (a division of Penguin Books Ltd)
Penguin Group (Australia), 250 Camberwell Road, Camberwell, Victoria 3124, Australia
(a division of Pearson Australia Group Pty Ltd)
Penguin Books India Pvt Ltd, 11 Community Centre, Panchsheel Park, New Delhi –
110 017, India
Penguin Group (NZ), 67 Apollo Drive, Rosedale, Auckland 0632, New Zealand (a division
of Pearson New Zealand Ltd)
Penguin Books (South Africa) (Pty) Ltd, 24 Sturdee Avenue, Rosebank, Johannesburg 2196,
South Africa

Penguin Books Ltd, Registered Offices: 80 Strand, London WC2R 0RL, England

10 9 8 7 6 5 4 3 2 1

Copyright © 2012 Mandy Hubbard

ISBN 978-1-59514-511-6

Library of Congress Cataloging-in-Publication Data is available

Printed in the United States of America

For Super Agent Zoe,
for being made of awesome.

PROLOGUE

He stares straight at me with that intense smile of his, and my heart lodges in my throat. "Your time is nearly up, Harper."

But it's not. It can't be. I scramble to my feet and lunge past him, tearing through the doorway and into the hallway. I race down the stairs so fast I trip over my own feet, grabbing at the banister to save myself. But as I yank myself to a stop, my body swings around and my shoulder slams into the wall. Tears, instant, well in my eyes as my breath disappears.

I turn back to the stairs and rush down the last few, to the first landing, but he's on me, grabbing my hair and yanking me back. I elbow him hard in the gut, and he grunts, releasing me as he stumbles down a few steps and doubles over. "You bitch," he grinds out.

He's blocking the stairs. When he stands again, anger blazing in his eyes, I whirl around and run back up the steps. I hit the top step, skidding on an area rug, barely saving myself.

I cross the empty bedroom, putting my foot through the windowsill just as he darkens the doorway. My dress rides up as I duck under the windowpane.

I'm only halfway out when he grabs my ankle, yanking hard. I scream and pull away, desperate. I lean back and kick violently, and my toe catches him on the chin. He curses and lets me go, and I fall onto the roof.

My heart, already scrambling, turns into a thunderous roar as I skid on a leaf, tumbling down the slope of the rain-slickened, moss-covered rooftop. There's no way to stop myself. I grab at anything in sight as I roll toward the edge, catching myself on an attic vent near the gutters, but it's not enough to stop my body's movement. My legs swing out over the edge and dangle toward the ground as rain slides past me, pours over the edge of the rotten soffits. The darkened clouds make it hard to see anything but the light blazing from his bedroom window.

I blink, trying to see through the raindrops, searching the roofline for his shadow.

"You're gonna regret that," he says, spitting the words as he steps into view, looming high above me. I must have split his lip, because blood trickles down his chin, making him look all the more sinister. He's on the roof above me, stepping slowly down toward the gutter. The muscles in my left arm tremble as my grip slides, until I'm hanging on with scarcely more than a fingertip.

I wonder if this is how my mom felt before she died. If she hung on desperately, hoping someone would come in time to save her. If she knew, as her fingers slid, that she was about to die.

I glance over my shoulder. There are no shrubs here, just too-long grass at least a dozen feet below. He takes another step toward me as the lightning flashes, and then my fingers slip, and I'm falling.

I land, hard, on the dampened, muddy earth below, the wind slamming from my lungs. I lie there, my mouth open like a fish gasping for air, the rain blinding me.

I'm alive.

I'm really alive.

When I finally regain my breath, I wipe my eyes free of the rain and look up at the roof, expecting to see him staring down at me.

But he's not there. I blink, searching the darkness for his face, but he's gone. I climb to my feet, still cradling my arm and gasping for air as I tear across the lawn and into the dark shadows of the woods, right when the door to the house slams open.

I'm not far into the tree line before I realize I'm no match for him. He's crashing through the brush with the speed of a raging bull. My foot slips in the mud and I go down, slamming to the ground just as I hear his strange laughter behind me.

My fingers touch something soft, hidden in the fallen leaves.

Heart hammering out of control, I push the leaves aside, and a scream dies in my throat. I cover my mouth with my hands and stare, gagging.

Two glassy, lifeless eyes stare back at me, deeply sunken, emotionless. His face is pale, waxy.

Dead.

It's his uncle, half-buried in the dampened earth under a big cedar tree.

He killed his uncle.

This whole time, he wasn't away on business, he was dead and rotting. The horror building in my chest, threatening to suffocate me, nearly makes me break down in sobs, but I can't. There's no time.

I climb to my feet, nausea swelling as I take off again, desperate, frantic for a savior, a safety net, something.

Anything.

The rain drips down my face, into my eyes, making it hard to see where I'm going. I leap over a tree root, the panic overwhelming me. My shoulder is numb now, completely devoid of pain.

He's getting closer with every second. He curses as a tree branch snaps, and I realize he's closing in on me. I push faster, my feet slipping as the rain deafens the sound of my muddy footsteps.

I'll never make it to the road, to another house. He lives so far away from anything. I have to hide or outsmart him or . . .

Or he'll kill me.

Lightning cracks across the sky, for the first time in many minutes, and then the thunder rumbles, slow and quiet at first, and then building until it drowns out everything else. I force my screaming muscles to move faster and faster as I careen through the trees like a bat out of hell.

Too late, I realize what I've done. Ahead and below, the Green River rages. There's a cliff. It must be two hundred feet tall, towering over the valley.

A beautiful vantage point for him to catch up, corner me.

He steps out of the tree line just a half-dozen feet away from me, smiling, his hair plastered to his face and his eyes dark. Tears swim in my vision, mingling with the raindrops sliding down my skin. It can't be this way.

It can't end like this.

CHAPTER ONE

One month earlier . . .

I stare out the windshield of the Jeep, watching two Holstein calves grazing in the field beyond the barbwire fence. One of them has a spot that looks like Mickey Mouse, and I can't stop gawking at it.

"Earth to Harper," comes the voice beside me.

I twist around and meet the dark brown eyes of Logan, my almost-boyfriend. We've been dating a few weeks now, but I'm not sure if we're exclusive. I'm afraid to ask because it seems too good to be true. Girls like me don't get boys like him. "Sorry, I was spacing out."

He fake pouts and I giggle, but the laughter dies in my throat when he leans toward me, his dark brown hair sliding onto his forehead. My eyes slip closed as our lips meet and his fingers tangle in my hair.

I lose all sense of time until someone—not Logan—clears

their throat and I jerk away.

"Ew," says a familiar voice. I turn and see my cousin Adam standing beside my door, smirking. I want to reach out and knock his ballcap off his head, like I used to when we were kids. When he wore caps every day, because he's always hated his more-red-than-brown hair.

I twist around and look through the back window of the Jeep, realizing Allie is standing there on the sidewalk, waiting.

"Oh, shut up," I say, but I'm grinning now, even as heat rises to my cheeks. Logan and I share a look—a look that tells me he's not at all embarrassed, which somehow makes me feel better—and then we unbuckle our seatbelts and slide out of the Jeep. I join Adam and his girlfriend—my best friend—Allie, who looks so unbelievably pleased I can't believe it doesn't hurt to smile so wide. Allie's been trying to hook me up with half the guys in a twenty-mile radius. She can't believe I'm dating the one guy she'd never met before our first date. Logan joins me on the sidewalk, playfully knocking shoulders with me.

"*Moo*," comes a familiar voice behind me.

The four of us turn to see Bick walking across the drive with that lazy, crooked smile of his, hands shoved deep into an old Carhartt jacket. Technically his name is Victor, but everyone calls him Bick. Partly because it rhymes with Vick, but mostly because he's the only guy at Enumclaw High School who can grow a full-fledged beard, and once Adam realized Bic was a razor, the name stuck.

"Moo yourself," I say, even though it probably doesn't make sense.

"Jealous of my mad skills, DQ?" he asks, his grin widening.

"You know it," I say. "Cattle calls are just so *impossible* to master."

"DQ?" Logan asks, interlacing his fingers with mine casually; warm butterflies swirl in my stomach. I wish we were alone right now.

"Dairy Queen," Allie supplies.

"Technically it's Dairy Princess," I mutter, even though I know resistance is futile.

"Yeah, didn't Harper tell you she was Dairy Princess last year?" Adam asks, turning toward the double doors behind him. He holds one open, and Allie slips by.

Logan looks down at me, and I blush, following Allie through the door. "No, she neglected to tell me that," he says. I can feel his eyes on me, but I resist meeting his gaze.

"Harper, I'm disappointed. This is first date material," Bick says, following Adam through the door, until we're all inside Frankie's Pizza.

"I guess it didn't come up," I say, inhaling the warm, delicious scent of tomato, cheese, and garlic. The place is packed with people from school. No surprise there. There's not exactly much else to do in Enumclaw, Washington. Except run for Dairy Princess—which is pretty much like a pageant with cow trivia thrown in for good measure—and come up with stupid nicknames for your friends.

We ignore the PLEASE WAIT TO BE SEATED sign and plunk down at the last available booth near the windows. Bick borrows a spare seat from another table and sits at the end. Last summer, before Logan moved here from Cedar Cove, Oregon, to start his junior year, Bick would have been sitting next to me, not in a spare chair at the end of the table.

I try not to notice how awkward it is, because Bick's not the sort of guy you give your sympathy to. He'd just mistake it for pity, and he doesn't do pity.

"I really don't feel like going to school tomorrow," Adam sighs.

"When do you ever?" I ask, kicking his foot under the table. He glares and kicks me back, like the big brother I never wanted.

"Hey. Some of us weren't born geniuses," Bick says, reaching over to pluck a menu out of the rack on the table, and then studying it as if he doesn't have the whole thing memorized already.

I roll my eyes. "An IQ of one-thirty-nine does not make me a genius."

"We know, we know. You're short one point," Allie says, her blonde curls bouncing as she shakes her head.

"Don't give me that! It was your idea for us to take the tests."

"You have an IQ of one-thirty-nine?" Logan asks, squeezing my knee under the table. "That's amazing."

"Mm-hmm," I say, looking out the window as a few orange leaves swirl in the autumn breeze before descending to the cold sidewalks. It's not like I'm some brainiac or something. I get good grades because I have a lot of time to study. When your best friend constantly ditches you to hang out with her boyfriend—who happens to be your cousin, the *other* person you normally hang out with—and your dad is too busy to notice you, there's not much else to do. "We did tests in August, a few weeks before I met you," I say, turning back to look at Logan again. "Allie still has some left over. You should take one," I say, grinning up at him. "You know, if you think you're an *actual* genius, and not just an almost-genius."

"Challenge accepted," he says.

I allow myself a small smirk. I knew he would agree. Logan's like that, never one to back down.

The waitress walks up, hands us each a glass of water and a wrapped straw. But before she can scamper away, Adam yanks the menu out of Bick's hand, putting it back into the table rack, and orders our usual two pizzas and a round of Cokes.

"You guys really like pepperoni, huh?" says Logan.

"Pepperoni, sausage, meatballs . . . really anything that combines meat with cheese," answers Bick, patting his stomach.

Allie rolls her eyes. "Um, right. Anyway. . . we still going to go to the haunted maze this weekend? I have to go to an out of town race with my parents on Saturday and Sunday, but Friday's free."

I immediately cringe. Somehow I'd hoped my friends would magically forget about our tradition.

"What haunted maze?" Logan asks, leaning forward. He rests his chin on my shoulder, so that his breath tickles my ear.

I try to act casual, ignoring the warm tingles sweeping down my back.

"There's this insanely creepy one in Buckley every year. Right off the highway," Adam says. He twists the paper at the end of his straw and then blows the wrapper off.

It sails across the table and narrowly misses Bick. He grabs it in midair and tosses it back onto the table. I dart a look at Logan, but he doesn't seem to mind their childish antics.

"I wanna go. I'm not sure if I have to milk, but I'll check," Bick says.

I nod. Bick and I both live on dairy farms. I have some basic chores, but my dad never makes me do the actual milkings. Right now I kind of wish I had the same excuse. "Have fun with that."

"You know it, DQ," he says, grinning.

"Count me in," Logan says, picking up his own straw. He shoots the wrapper at me, and it somehow slips into my shirt.

When he gives me a mischievous, flirty smile, I know he did it on purpose, and I shake my head, fighting the heat rising in my cheeks. "Don't even think about it," I say, batting his hand away and fishing the paper out of my top.

He smiles a much-too-innocent puppy dog smile that's impossible to resist. I stare back at his dark, deep brown eyes for a long moment, until Bick clears his throat, shaking us from our all-too-public flirting session.

What were we talking about? Oh, right . . . "I don't know about the maze. I feel creeped out enough already with the stuff going on in town. I don't think I'm up for it."

Adam shrugs. "Oh, come on. It's just some pranks."

"It *is* kind of weird," Allie says. "The police blotter has actual crime in it."

"It's not really that weird. It's just some idiot with too much time on their hands," Bick says, leaning back in his chair so that it's balancing on two legs.

"Bloody bones left in mailboxes is not a joke," I say, the revulsion evident in my voice.

"They were cow bones," Adam reminds me.

Allie makes a disgusted face. "Yeah, but you know it must have looked like they could've been human, because the old lady called the cops."

I nod. "I don't care what it was; I wouldn't want to find it in *my* mailbox."

"It was probably just that guy who was peeping in windows. They arrested him three days ago, and nothing since," Adam says.

"The whole point is that there *was* a Peeping Tom," I say, sipping my water. "We're not supposed to have those in Enumclaw."

"Wasn't the Green River Killer from around here?" Logan asks, spinning his straw around in his glass, so that the ice swirls.

I shake my head. "No, he lived in Kent. I mean, the Green River runs just north of town, by your house, but I don't think they found any bodies in that part."

"They found one near the golf course," Allie says, snatching her unwrapped straw back from Adam when he tries to take it.

I shudder. The golf course is only about a mile down the highway—the highway I can see from where I'm sitting. "Yeah, and who knows?" I say. "They said he killed so many people he lost count at seventy. There could still be bodies out there somewhere."

Bick lets his chair drop back down on all four legs. "It was twenty years ago. The guy is serving, like, fifty life sentences. Nothing ever happens here anymore."

"I dunno. I guess," I say, twisting Logan's errant straw wrapper in my hands. "I still don't want to go to the maze. Why willingly creep myself out when someone else is doing a fine job with it already?"

"That's what makes it more fun," Adam says.

"We haven't missed it in six years. You can't skip it now," Allie adds.

"Besides, I'll protect you," Logan adds, slinging an arm around me and giving me a totally cheestastic grin.

I meet Bick's stare and roll my eyes—it's impossible not to—but I actually find the sentiment kind of charming. "Fine, fine. I'll go. But for the record, I am doing so under duress."

Our sodas arrive then, and we fall silent as we overload on caffeine. By the time we've devoured the pizza, it's pitch-dark outside. We push through the double doors and out into the brisk October night. I zip my jacket up to my chin and accept Logan's hand when he puts it out for me, his skin warm against the cool autumn air.

Then we pause as Bick steps off the curb. "See y'all tomorrow," he says, crossing the lot. His dairy is the one next door,

13

with the Mickey-Mouse-spotted-calf, so he's walking home, across the grassy fields.

"Bye," I say, turning to Logan's Jeep, my hand on the passenger door.

"Have a good night!" Allie calls out.

We say our goodbyes to Allie and Adam, and then it's a short drive to the old farmhouse I call home. Along the way, we pass cattail-filled ditches, sprawling dairy farms, and narrow county roads. Then Logan pulls into the gravel driveway, parking near the edge of the back patio.

I look up at the house. It's dark. Empty. Just like always. My dad's probably already asleep. He does the first milking of the day at, like, four o'clock, so it's rare that he stays up past nine.

A few years ago, before my mom died and Dad got so busy, he used to leave me notes before he went to bed, or in the morning before he disappeared into the barns and fields. Just little ones, with smiley faces or short messages like, "Have a great day!" and "Good luck on your test!"

But he stopped doing that a long time ago. You know that saying about two ships passing in the night? That's us. Now it's always me and that house and total silence.

Logan walks with me across the cracked cement patio, to the back screen door. I turn back to him, take in the seductive darkness of his eyes. Behind him, sprawling green pastures stretch out below the clear velvet sky, as a smattering of stars twinkles to life.

He smiles, in that way that's *ours*, and pulls me closer, his kiss whisper soft. I like the seductive feel of his lips curling upward as I kiss him back.

He rests his forehead against mine, and I close my eyes, breathing him in, memorizing the feeling of being this close.

I've never had this before—such an intoxicating relationship. A guy who seems to want me in the same way I want him. The complete inability to think clearly when he's this close, and the tantalizing hope that he feels the same way.

"Can I ask you a question?"

I nod, and he squeezes my hand.

"We're exclusive, right?"

My eyes flutter open and I stare straight into the dark depths of his. "Um, are we?"

He looks down at me, a smile playing at the edges of his lips, making me want to kiss him again just so I can *feel* his smile, not just see it. "Do you want to be?"

I swallow and nod. He pulls me against him, and I close my eyes, resting my cheek against his shoulder. "Then let's. I don't want to share you with anyone."

"Okay," I say, oddly breathless.

"Your enthusiasm is staggering," he says.

I laugh, slipping my arms around his waist and giving him a squeeze. "Sorry. You just make me nervous." I giggle, and it sounds stupid and silly. But he must not take it that way because when I pull away, he's beaming at me, smiling in a way that makes me want to melt into nothingness. Beautiful, blissful nothingness.

"I'll take that as a compliment," he says, kissing the top of my head.

I reluctantly let go, and he steps away, walking to his Jeep just as I'm pulling open the screen door.

"Hey!" he calls out. I turn around. "Sweet dreams."

Warmth unfurls inside me. "Like I'm going to be able to sleep tonight, thanks to you," I say, grinning. "But sweet dreams to you too."

And then I slip into the dark, lonely house.

CHAPTER TWO

The next morning, I'm sitting at the chipped Formica counter when someone bangs on the back door. I jump, sloshing the milk in my cereal bowl. I can't see him, but I know without looking that it's Logan because he's picked me up every day for school for the last two weeks, and now it's this unspoken thing, as dependable as the incessant rain at this time of year.

"Come in!" I holler, slurping another spoonful of cereal as he steps through the door.

"'Morning, beautiful." Whenever he stands in this house, it's a reminder of our differences. He's wearing crisp, practically new jeans and a button-down, the sleeves rolled up to expose his muscular forearms. As he leans a hip against our countertop, crossing his arms, I forget to swallow the food in my mouth.

I blush. How can he call me beautiful when he's dressed like that and I'm in torn blue jeans and an old Darigold T-shirt? When my nickname is DQ and his might as well be GQ?

"Coffee?" I point to the coffeemaker, full to the brim. I started it ten minutes ago in anticipation of Logan's arrival. When he smiles at me, those dark eyes trained right on mine, I'm glad I didn't forget.

I slurp another spoonful of cereal and watch as Logan pours coffee into the mug I'd set out for him. He picks the cup up to his lips and my stomach lurches—along the edge, there's a chip the size of a dime. It makes the whole thing look really cheap and country, even for me. Why didn't I spot that before?

Logan won't care, but I do. I shouldn't be so irritated by something that stupid, but can't things—for once—be simple and clean and perfect? Like they probably would be if Mom were still around and Dad noticed anything inside this house?

I guess Logan doesn't notice or maybe he's just too nice to say anything because the next thing out of his mouth is a compliment. "This is so good. It's criminal that my uncle only buys decaf."

I don't tell him that my dad does, too. That I bought coffee especially for him. I wonder if he'd think it was silly or sweet, if he knew.

I decide on sweet. I slide back the stool and place my cereal bowl into the sink. It lands with a heavy clunk of ceramic on metal. "We should probably go. I don't want to be late for politics and I need to run out to the barn to get lunch money from my dad."

He follows me through to the back porch, which is littered with a dozen pairs of rubber boots. The screen door slaps shut behind us as I walk across the gravel driveway, dodging mud puddles that never seem to dry up, except in August. Logan fires up the Jeep as I climb the cement stairs to the milking parlor.

I slide the wooden door sideways on its track, flecks of peeling gray paint sticking to my palm. The methodical pulsing noises of the equipment greet me as I step into the parlor. There aren't any cows here yet, so the cement is washed clean, and I don't have to dodge any cowpies.

My dad is in the pit, restocking the old, frayed washcloths that have already seen a hundred milkings. He smiles when he sees me, and I smile back without meaning to. It's hard to be mad at him when he doesn't disappear on purpose. He's simply overwhelmed.

"Feed the calves?" he asks, meeting my eyes.

I look away, stare up at the chalkboard where a few cows' three-digit identification numbers are listed. The cows on antibiotics, whose milk can't go into the tank with the others'. "Yeah." I get up before six in order to do a few chores before school. By the time Logan shows up, I've been up for an hour and a half. I'm always paranoid that by the time I climb into his Jeep, I smell like a cow. I mean, I take a shower and everything, but still. A guy like him can't be used to farmyard smells. He's too . . . perfect. Clean, crisp . . .

Amazing.

"I gave the wild-white on the end some sulfa. She didn't look like she was doing too well," I say, feeling awkward. My dad and I hardly talk these days.

He nods. "I'll check on her when I'm done in here."

"Cool. Can I get some lunch money?"

"Oh." He blinks. "Yeah. Sorry. I meant to leave it on the counter."

He digs into his pockets, producing a crumpled dollar bill and five quarters. Enough for a soda and the pizza pocket I get every day.

"Thanks, Dad." I nod and turn on my heel. Years ago, just after my mom died, I might have tried to hug him, but not anymore. It only took a few wooden embraces for me to realize that he wasn't going to try to fill my mom's role as the resident family hugger. So for the last six years, we've kind of just kept to ourselves—him in the parlor or the barns or the fields, and me in the house, sticking his dinner in the fridge before I do my homework or go hang out with friends.

I climb the ladder at the end of the pit, and through the dingy window, I see Logan's red Jeep rolling to a stop. It occurs to me that he really *gets* what it's like to go without a parent. It's one of those things he and I have in common. That we're basically all alone family-wise. Only difference is that Logan lives with his uncle because *both* of his parents passed away. Then again, I live with a father who barely speaks to me about anything other than milking cows, so it's almost the same thing.

I take another look at my dad's bent form, sigh, and then shove the door shut behind me. The pulsating sound of the vacuum pump quickly dies out as I scurry to Logan's Jeep. He's waiting for me like the knight in shining armor that I imagine him to be. I roll my shoulders, forcing all thoughts of my mottled family life from my mind, and climb into the passenger seat, slamming the door behind me.

We leave my driveway and head right, toward Enumclaw High School. Sitting alongside Logan immediately makes me feel more relaxed, calmer. He squeezes my hand.

Then suddenly he's distracted.

"Look," he says, pointing out the windshield. "What is that?"

I lean forward and look up, to where a lime-green aircraft is gliding above us. "It's an ultralight."

"A what?"

"They're these super light airplanes. Up close it looks like a three-wheeled Go Kart attached to wings. There's an airstrip down the street, so they fly over my house a lot."

"That's so cool," Logan exclaims, the enthusiastic longing evident in his voice.

I snort. "If you have a death wish."

Logan darts a glance at me, then stares back up at the airplane. "You think so? I'd love to fly in one of those someday."

"No way," I say, shaking my head quickly. "It's on my list."

"What is on what list?"

I feel my cheeks redden. "Uh, flying. It's on my list of fears."

Logan coasts to a halt at a stop sign and then turns to me. "You have a list of fears?"

I nod. "Um, yeah. I mean, sort of. Okay, yeah." I cringe and turn away, watching the airplane high above us. Only I would make a brand-new boyfriend think I was meant for the loony bin.

Oddly enough, though, Logan doesn't seem fazed. He places his thumb against my cheek and gently shifts my gaze back to him. "How many things are on your list?" he asks tenderly.

"Ten."

"And flying is?"

"Number ten."

A car honks behind us, so Logan pulls away from the sign. "Are you going to tell me the rest?"

"No way," I say. "I didn't even mean to tell you that one. Allie and Adam know I'm a chicken, but they don't know I have an actual *list*. You can't tell anyone."

"Hey," Logan says, and I turn back to meet his eyes. "I won't tell them. You can trust me."

I swallow and nod, realizing I do. Trust him, that is.

"But you have to share the rest. How else am I supposed to be sure you confront all of your so-called fears?"

I shake my head. "It's not a bucket list."

"Well it should be. Any person who cares enough to keep track of the things that they're afraid of obviously thinks about said things. Right?"

I give him a blank stare.

Logan takes this as his cue to continue. "Come on, Harper. Conquer your fears. Seize the moment. Carpe diem or whatever."

I laugh. "You swear you won't tell Adam or Allie? Or Bick? Adam already thinks I'm a wet blanket. And I don't know

22

what Allie thinks. Probably the same thing."

"She does not," he says.

"I don't know. She's way more adventurous than me and doesn't understand why I'm not into riding horses and stuff."

Logan adjusts his rearview mirror. "It's a deal, on one condition."

"What's that?"

"You have to tell me the rest of your list."

I smile and, feeling more adventurous than I do ordinarily, decide there's little harm in playing his game. I trace my finger down along his arm, letting my fingers tangle with his just long enough to give his hand a squeeze. Then I let go so he can shift gears. "Ask me tomorrow, and maybe I'll tell you another one."

He bursts into an ear-to-ear grin, excitement and satisfaction swirling in his eyes. Then he flicks a blinker on and turns on Cole Street, the main drag through town. "Fair enough."

The base of my neck grows hot and tingles creep up my spine as I turn back toward the window in an attempt to maintain a calm and collected exterior, at least temporarily. I watch as we glide past our little town newspaper, the post office, antique shops, and a few modest mom-and-pop restaurants.

I'm still staring out the window, my mind wandering, when Logan abruptly hits the brakes. The tires screech on the concrete. I sit up straighter, peering out the windshield, to the view that has Logan dumbstruck.

Birds. Hundreds of them.

And they're all dead.

CHAPTER THREE

Logan stares for a moment longer, then turns the Jeep and pulls into one of the last available parking stalls in the jam-packed gravel lot. We climb out, but we don't step much farther than the front bumper of his car.

In the next lot—the cement one where all the seniors normally park—two janitors in coveralls drag a heavy, overflowing garbage can to the Dumpster. It takes both of them to lift it and tip it over. The bird corpses flow out in a river of feathers.

I gulp, swallowing the nausea welling at the gruesome sight. Logan places his arm around me, and I force myself to breathe as we stand there, side by side, staring and silent.

The janitors slide the empty garbage can back across the lot, pick up their shovels, and resume scooping up dead birds.

Suddenly, Logan finds his voice. "It's not even one kind. It's crows, pigeons, swallows. Everything."

I shiver, and Logan reaches over, rubbing my arm as I stare

out at the carnage. The bodies litter the whole parking lot, dot the front lawn, sprawl across the cement pathways. Everywhere I look, another bird. The scraping sound of shovel-on-cement punctuates the silence.

I shield my eyes from the early morning sun and watch as one of the janitors scoops up another shovelful of birds, tossing them into the garbage can. Over and over, he scoops and tosses, but it's hardly made a dent. Barely a third of the parking lot is cleared.

"There must be a thousand of them," Logan says. I could be wrong, but I swear his voice wavers, just a bit.

I decide to ignore it. If he wants to put on a brave face for me, who am I to stop him?

"It's too much. . . ." He continues, trailing off. The birds have clearly upset him more than he wants to let on.

"I wonder what happened," I say, my voice low. I clear my throat, feeling strangely shaky. They're birds. *Just birds.*

Logan steadies himself, then looks me in the eye. "It's almost like what happened in Arkansas."

"Huh?"

"Thirty minutes before midnight on New Year's Eve, a thousand birds dropped from the sky. Dead."

A chill winds down my spine. "What was wrong with them?"

Logan glances at the grisly sight, then turns back to me just as quickly.

"They never figured it out."

• • •

"Meet up with you in politics?" Logan asks as we step through the double doors of the school building. "I need to go to my locker."

"Sure. See you in a few." I duck into the girls' bathroom, wanting a moment to blink away the vision of all those dead birds. I check beneath the stalls and am grateful to discover that they're empty. I breathe a sigh of relief, then turn on the faucet and wash my hands, splashing the cold water over my face, happy I don't wear mascara. I rub my eyes, then look at myself in the mirror. I really need to leave for class.

Suddenly, I imagine the sink filling up with feathers and dead birds dropping from the ceiling. *Not real, they're not real,* I tell myself. I wouldn't be this freaked out if it weren't for the cow bones and the Peeping Tom and all the other horror-movie stuff that's been happening.

Still, though, the memory of all those lifeless bodies taunts me. There wasn't any blood or scattered feathers or anything. They just . . . landed there. Dead. Like their hearts all gave out at the same moment, spontaneously.

My own heart beats rapidly, feeling as if it's going to explode out of my chest. I take deep breaths, in and out, and another image pops into my mind: Logan, silencing his own fears to be there for me, to be the boyfriend, the person, I needed. I force myself to focus on him, only him. My heart stills. Then my heavy breathing evens out.

I turn off the water.

After a quiet moment in the bathroom, I finally feel as if I'm ready to face the rest of the world. I go to my locker to dump my math book. Balancing the book in one hand, I twist the lock with the other and, when I swing it open, a red rose tumbles out, landing on my feet.

It's gorgeous, the crimson petals just beginning to bloom. I scoop it up and, taking a big breath of it, I feel all warm and fluttery. Logan didn't need to go to his locker at all. He needed to go to *mine*.

A black ribbon is looped around the stem at least a dozen times, and a small scrap of paper is tucked into it. I slide the paper out and unroll it.

Watch out for thorns.

Aw. That's sort of sweet. Kind of weird, I guess, but sweet.

I take another sniff of it and then slide it back into my locker for safe keeping, slamming the door before walking to first period.

I plunk down next to Logan in my usual spot in the back row, turning toward him. "Thank you," I say.

He smiles at me. The discomfort he showed outside is gone, replaced by his usual easy confidence. "For?"

I grin back, feeling oddly bashful. "Being an awesome boyfriend."

Boyfriend. It's the first time I've said that aloud. I like the way it sounds.

He beams. "Of course."

I look up in time to see Madison Vaughn waltzing through the door, then quickly dart my eyes away. For some stupid reason, I always act as if she's a Tyrannosaurus rex, and as long as I don't move, she won't notice me. By some cruel twist of fate, Logan and I ended up seated right behind her, which means I get to stare at her gleaming red hair for an hour every morning, thinking of what she did to Bick.

She plunks down in her seat and twists around, leaning an elbow on my desk and smiling coyly at Logan, her green eyes bright and pretty, framed by thick lashes. Madison's the kind of girl who could model Halloween costumes like "Sexy Firefighter" and "Sexy Nurse" without breaking a sweat. It doesn't matter what she's wearing, she's always alluring, the kind of attractiveness that makes me wonder how Logan could see anything in me when girls like her exist. "So, how was your weekend?" she asks Logan.

"Not bad," Logan says. "Yours?"

"Kinda lonely," she says, pouting as she stares at my boyfriend. Her lips are so perfectly glossed she belongs on a Covergirl spread. I wonder if she reapplied her makeup for this exact moment.

I sit back and cross my arms, acting as if she doesn't intimidate me. "Seriously, Madison? I'm right here." I tap on my desk, trying not to cringe at the dirt under my nails.

She turns as if just now noticing me. "I'm not sure what you're talking about," she says. *Her* nails are polished a pretty, pale pink.

I grind my teeth.

Fortunately, our teacher, Mr. Patricks, interrupts before I have to choose between defending the honor of my relationship and risking detention. "All right, guys, let's settle down and talk elections," he says, stepping to the right of the dry-erase board.

Madison, to my relief, twists back around and turns her attention to the teacher instead of *my boyfriend*.

"To tie in with our unit on elections, we're going to launch a very exciting new project!" He waits for a collective expression of awe, but no one speaks. "For the next few weeks, we'll be running political campaigns within the class. You'll be divided into two groups, one Democratic and one Republican. Each group will choose one student from their members to represent them as their candidate, and the rest of you will act as campaign managers or workers. Candidates must conform to the ideals of their respective, real-life parties. Members of the winning party will receive twenty bonus points on their midterms." He pauses again, smiling smugly as he finally gets the reaction he wanted. Cheers echo out throughout the class. "So choose your candidates wisely."

I lean in closer. The assignment actually sounds kind of interesting. Mr. Patricks is impossibly boring when he lectures, always pausing dramatically as if we're all dying of suspense to find out how many hours it took to sign the Declaration of Independence. I'd much rather work on a project.

Mr. Patricks continues, his self-satisfied smile never leaving his face. "Each group will run a full campaign, including advertising and a speech, and secondary classes will be the ones to vote."

I feel someone poke me, and look to my left. Logan immediately catches my eye. He also seems to be on the edge of his seat.

Mr. Patricks walks to the front of the room, picks up a

bowl from his desk, and marches over to the first row. "These scraps of paper," he says, waiting as a girl in the front pulls a torn slip out, "will say whether you are with the Democratic or Republican party."

He continues throughout the room, pausing at each student long enough for them to grab a scrap of paper. "I expect you to fully research and understand your party, and develop a strategy that mirrors its real life campaigns."

Logan grabs a piece of paper and moves to uncrumple it before suddenly hesitating. "What if we want to run an independent campaign?"

Mr. Patricks stops. "What are you proposing?"

Logan shrugs. "If you want to accurately reflect real-life elections, shouldn't you include at least one independent candidate? He or she could have a much smaller campaign crew."

Mr. Patricks studies Logan. "And are you volunteering to be that candidate, Mr. Townsend?"

"Actually," Logan says, his eyes flickering over to me. "I was thinking I could manage the campaign. Harper here would be the stronger candidate."

My jaw drops. How am *I* the stronger candidate? I can't talk in front of more than three people without freaking out. There's no way I can campaign.

Mr. Patricks's lips sorta screw to the side as he considers Logan's idea. He glances between me and Logan, his eyebrows narrowed. He so did not see this coming.

"Very well. There are twenty-six students in this class, and twenty-four gives us an even number for each of the two primary parties. You two can run an independent campaign," Mr. Patricks says, waving his hand over our corner of the room. He then turns and strides back to the front, depositing the bowl on his desk along the way.

Logan winks at me as soon as Mr. Patricks turns back to the dry-erase board, scribbling down our first deadlines.

My pulse races. Did Logan come up with this whole thing just so that he and I could spend more time by ourselves? That's so conniving . . . *and so perfect.*

"You guys have this period to determine which student from each group will be the candidate, and then develop the basic platform around that student. I expect to have the candidates' names by the end of class. Please have one representative from each party pick up this flier, which outlines your campaign responsibilities." He pauses, glancing our way. "And you two—independent candidates don't have the same resources as the major parties. You're restricted by half on each of the bullet points on this flier. That means fewer campaign posters, fewer giveaways." He turns back to the class. "Go ahead and rearrange your desks and get to work."

The screeching sounds of chairs on tile fill the room as everyone shuffles around, matching up with those in their group.

I stare pointedly at Logan.

He just grins back, his eyes glimmering. "So how do you like me now? Snagging us some alone time, just you, me, and a little campaign action. Not too bad, huh?"

I don't let myself give in to his adorableness, because he's missing a major point: I am not a good candidate.

"Public speaking?" he says questioningly.

I narrow my eyes.

He sits up straight in his chair, crossing his arms and meeting my gaze with a triumphant smile. "Tell me it's not on your list."

My lips part but I just stare for a long moment, stunned.

His grin widens. "What number is it?"

I clear my throat. "Seven. It's fear number seven."

My mother was an amazing public speaker. She taught non-credit art courses at the local community college and could lecture to a hundred people without breaking a sweat. I, on the other hand, not so much. I stuttered my way through a one-minute answer in the Dairy Princess competition and nearly lost the whole shebang.

He beams. "Oooh . . . jumping three!"

I ignore his lame attempt at a joke. "How did you know?" I ask.

He leans forward, pulling my hands onto his desk, intertwining his fingers with mine. "That one was a given. I know you better than you think I do."

Heat rises to my cheeks. "Really?"

"Yup. And I'm going to break you out of your little box yet." Logan bangs his fist against the desk, as if to say that's the end of it.

Even though I'm still freaking out, I can't resist teasing him. "I dunno about that. Braver men have tried."

"Ooh, is that a challenge?"

"No. I—"

"Well, Harper Bennett, I accept," he says, grinning.

I can't help but smile back at him. "We're going to lose. You would have been a *much* better candidate."

"Nonsense! You're going to be amazing."

And in the glow of his smile, I almost believe it.

Two and a half hours later, I'm sitting in the commons at lunch, picking at my usual pizza pocket. I'm sandwiched on a long bench between Bick and Logan, across from Allie and Adam.

"Oh look, it's the hick clique," a nasal voice calls out.

Madison.

I swallow before slowly turning around to acknowledge her. As I do so, I notice that Bick has averted his eyes and that he refuses to look at her. Seeing him stiffen only angers me further.

"I thought you'd like to know that they figured out how the birds died," Madison says. She waits, but no one takes the bait. "Turns out they heard you were coming," she says, staring right at me, "and they preferred suicide to seeing your face." She smirks.

I swallow, frantically searching for a snappy response, but nothing comes, and her smirk turns into a self-satisfied grin. "I'm really looking forward to the masquerade," she says, pausing for dramatic effect, her eyes boring right into mine. "You know . . . so you'll be wearing a mask and *I* don't have to see your face either." And then she strolls away, her heels clacking on the tiles.

"Why is she such a bitch?" I ask, turning back around. It takes everything I have not to look over and ask Bick if he's doing okay. He's not the sort of guy who likes to admit weakness, and I know he doesn't want that kind of attention.

Besides, he's Bick. Of course he's okay. He's made of steel or something.

"Because she's ugly and has no soul?" Allie says, making me snort. And *that* is why she's my closest friend.

For a long time, Adam was the closest thing I had to a best friend, and he's my cousin, so it's practically required. Then the three of us—me, Adam, and Allie—shared a fourth grade classroom, and we became a trio. We were inseparable, like the Three Musketeers. Bick came along in junior high. He and I live on dairies, Adam on a heifer ranch, and Allie at thoroughbred racing stables. We were pretty much fated to become joined at the hip. Between the four of us, we had hundreds of acres to explore and call our own.

I look up to smile at Allie—she always knows just what to say to ensure I forget about Madison—but her eyes are trained on Adam, and the smile falls away.

Things changed last year, when Adam and Allie got together. Then it started to become awkward. Bick's almost always busy with his parents' dairy, so I was kind of feeling like the third wheel until I started dating Logan.

If it wasn't for him, I'm not sure what I'd do.

"Do you think they actually figured out how the birds died?" Bick asks.

"I saw a news van out there during second period," Allie

34

says. "It seems like it's a big deal. They'll figure it out, right?"

Adam balls up his napkin and tosses it on his tray. "I heard they kept a few of them for autopsy, or something, but they don't expect to determine the cause of death."

"But why wouldn't they figure it out?" Bick asks.

"They never did in Arkansas," Logan says.

"Or Sweden," Adam says.

"Sweden?" I ask, taking a bite of my pizza pocket.

"Yeah, we talked about it in my science class," Adam says. "Mr. Yarborough has this thing for weird science. Anyway, I guess this has happened before. All over the world. The other cases were different, though."

"Different how?" I ask, setting down my lunch. I'm suddenly not so hungry.

"In Arkansas, it was all blackbirds. In Sweden, it was all jackdaws, whatever that is," Adam says, reaching over to tear a piece off my pizza pocket. "The point, though, is that all the birds were the same species."

"But in our case, it was a ton of different kinds," I say, finally getting it. "I wonder why?"

Logan leans forward. "It's supposed to be a sign of the apocalypse," he says. "I mean, if you're into the Bible. Or conspiracy theories."

"Great, well, at least we have that to look forward to," Allie says, rolling her eyes. "Just make sure it doesn't happen before the masquerade, will you?"

"Masquerade?" Logan asks. "The one Madison was just talking about?"

"Yep," Allie says, bouncing around in her chair. "She's head of the committee. Every year EHS does this totally over-the-top Halloween Masquerade. People get really into it."

"So are we going?" Logan asks, turning to me.

Familiar heat creeps up my neck. "Um, are you asking me?"

He grins. "Miss Harper Bennett, will you please consider accompanying me to said Halloween Masquerade?"

Adam, Allie, Bick, and Logan all stare at me. "Um, sure," I say.

Logan turns to Allie. "Count us in."

"Awesome! Now we can go costume shopping together!" she says, setting her sandwich back down on her tray. "We only have a few weeks, so we should totally start planning."

"Sounds good." I turn to Bick. "Are you going?"

He glances up from his plate and shrugs. "Nah. I think I'll pass."

"How can you *not* go?" Allie asks. "You have to."

"It's cool," he says, avoiding her eyes. "The girl I wanted to ask is already going with someone else."

"Oh," Allie says. "Sorry."

Bick stands up with his empty tray. "Like I said. It's cool. I gotta head out." He takes a few steps toward the doors, and we all watch him go as he walks away.

"Do you think he's still not over Madison?" Allie asks.

Logan twists around and stares at Allie, wide-eyed. "Madison?"

I nod. "Yeah, they dated last spring. That's why we universally hate her. We can't *not*. She kind of messed with his head."

"She seemed like she was actually into him," Adam says. "At least at first."

"*Maybe* she was," Allie says. "But in the end she still screwed him over, so it doesn't really matter."

I nod. "She dumped him at Tolo. It's this casual dance, but you have to wear matching outfits. She made him wear these designer jeans and a button-down, stuff *she* likes, but anyone with two brain cells could tell it wasn't Bick's style." I frown and look back at the doors, where Bick disappeared. "So you can imagine how awkward it must have been for Bick when he and Madison are dressed like twins, and then everyone sees her grinding all over Trevor Reynolds."

"Ouch." Logan glances over his shoulder, at where Madison sits with her group of plastic friends. "I can't picture them together."

I nod. "Yeah, we've all been wondering if it was some kind of game to her. You know, like a bet. Date the redneck for a couple months, dress him up, and dump him. If her plan was to devastate him, it worked."

"Anyway," Allie says, brightening again. "Back to the costumes for the masquerade. They've gotta be killer."

CHAPTER FOUR

Friday finally arrives, and with it, our group trip to the haunted maze. I'm considering calling Allie to say that I've come down with a sudden case of food poisoning when Logan swings into my driveway, the perennial mud puddles splashing under his Jeep's big tires. I pull my jacket on and slip into a worn pair of cowboy boots. Allie loves pointing out that I own cowboy boots, yet I refuse to ride horses. But whatever, they're cuter than rubber boots. With my skinny jeans, even Allie would approve. She did pick them out, after all.

I cross the back patio, not waiting for Logan to do his usual jump-out-and-open-my-door thing. Instead, I just climb in and lean over the gap between our seats, brushing my lips against his, embracing my newfound ability to kiss him without feeling totally freaked out and nervous.

"Lovely weather we're having," Logan says, peering out the window at the overcast sky.

"Yep. Welcome to October in Enumclaw."

He eyeballs the clouds, which have grown darker since I've been inside. "You think it'll get worse?"

"Nah. We'll be fine. Bad weather never lasts long. I'm sure we'll get a dry patch while we're in the cornfield."

"Okay. As long as you don't think it's going to get too nasty. You ready?" he asks, sliding the key into the ignition.

"Yep."

"So what's this thing like, anyway?" Logan asks, shifting into reverse. I watch him as he does so, and my eyes catch on the end of the stick shift: it's a soccer ball. I stare at it for a long moment, trying to remember if it's always been a soccer ball, or if it was something else before. I honestly can't remember Logan ever even telling me that he was interested in soccer. . . .

"Haaaarrrrrppppeeerrrr?" he intones, interrupting my train of thought.

I blink. "What? Oh, uh, the haunted maze? It's pretty freaky."

"Really? It's actually scary?"

The windows fog over as we pull out of the driveway, so I lean forward and crank the heater up. "Uh, yeah. There's a reason I didn't want to go."

Logan shifts up. "I won't let anything happen to you."

Somehow the idea of doing the maze together makes it seem easier. "Thanks."

"You never did tell me what number eight or nine is," he says.

"I was hoping you'd forget!" I say, grinning.

Logan glances over at me, sliding his hand off the gearshift and onto my knee. He squeezes it as a soft smile plays on his lips.

"Well, number nine is horseback riding," I say.

He raises a brow. "Doesn't Allie live on a horse farm?"

"Racing stables. Yeah. They have like two dozen horses, but most of them are broodmares or stallions. Not exactly backyard ponies."

"I see. And I'm guessing she tries to convince you to ride?"

I nod. "Yeah. It drives her crazy, but if you saw the horses at her house, you wouldn't climb aboard either. Sometimes she exercises the horses in the winter, when Emerald Downs—that's the closest racetrack—is closed. Allie has this big practice track at her house. It's like a half-mile, or something. And she's totally amazing. She just flies around the track. I could never do that."

"You could if you wanted to," Logan says. "Or you could take lessons on horses less likely to run away with you." He pauses. "Not that I'd blame any horses that wanted to do that."

I chuckle. "Are you really speaking about horses, Mr. Townsend?"

Logan's lips curl into a devilish grin. "Eh, more like from personal experience . . ."

I shake my head, but I can't keep the smile from my face. "I dunno. Like I said, the list isn't a challenge. It's just a list."

I don't mention that it's all inspired by my mother. I can't let go of if I don't want to end up like her . . .

"Well, maybe *I* think it's a challenge," he says, his eyebrows dancing like he's The Rock or something.

I burst out laughing. "And I guess you like challenges, huh?" I shove him playfully.

"You know, only if they involve a certain girlfriend of mine."

Heat rushes through me. There's that word again: *girlfriend*. The more I hear it, the more I like it.

The conversation falls away as we turn on the main drag, cut through town, and hit Highway 410. A few minutes later, we're crossing the old steel bridge over the White River. I watch the river, swollen and frothy, raging below us, and my mind drifts back to the conversation we had about the Green River Killer at Frankie's Pizza.

Hmm . . . I wonder why he picked the Green River for all seventy or eighty bodies. The White River is just as inaccessible. It winds up into the Cascade Mountain range, same as the Green River.

I blink away the morbid thoughts, turning back to the highway. Logan shifts down, pulling into the packed entry to the farm-stand-slash-pumpkin-patch-slash-corn-maze just as the clouds give in, and a misty rain coats the windshield.

"You sure the weather's going to be okay?"

"Yeah, don't worry about it. It'll drizzle for a bit, maybe, but we'll be fine. Unless you think you'll melt," I tease.

He pokes me playfully, and I laugh as we unbuckle our seatbelts.

Cars fill the field, which has been mowed low so that it can double as a parking lot, and we find an available space at the end. As we climb out of the car, the image of a different lot—sprinkled with dead, feathered bodies—swarms my vision.

I blink away the mental picture. I'm just psyching myself out, thinking of killers and dead birds, because I'm freaked out over the maze. "There's Adam's car," I say, pointing to his battered Samurai.

We walk across the grass, meeting Adam in the middle of the squishy field. Allie appears from the passenger seat, frantically pulling the hood of her rain poncho over her freshly styled, bouncy blonde curls.

"Scared of a little humidity?" I joke. At least that's one thing that doesn't bother me.

"Uh, yeah." She nods. "I know it's ridiculous, but you know what happens—I turn into a total Chia Pet."

I shake my head and give her a hug.

"Anyway, you look cute," she says.

"Thanks!" I do a little twirl. "You were right. They don't look like stretch pants."

She laughs and bumps her hip into mine. "You really need to take my fashion advice more often."

"Yeah, yeah, I know."

"Ahem . . ." Adam clears his throat. "Girls, I hate to interrupt your little fashion show, but the haunted maze awaits!"

I look around, counting up who's already in attendance. "Wait, Bick isn't coming?"

"Nah," says Logan as he places his palm on the small of my back. "He had to work."

I glance at him quizzically. "And he told you?"

Logan shrugs. "Guess he likes me."

"Huh. Wonder why." I move to elbow him, but he's too fast. He grabs me in a big bear hug and starts tickling me.

"Enough! Enough! I surrender," I call out through a fit of giggles.

"You better," teases Logan.

"Uh, guys, there are other people here . . ." Allie chimes in.

I stand up straight, fixing the belt on my coat—it came undone during the tickle session—and immediately agree. "Okay, okay. Whatever you say." Secretly, though, I'm just a little bit happy that Allie was the one who felt out of the loop for once . . . even if it meant that I had to make a fool of myself in public.

The four of us cross the muddy field, and Logan and Adam buy the tickets. We follow them, and a flow of people, to a corn maze behind the farm stand. Shrieks float out from the corn stalks as darkness falls.

Allie and Adam walk, hand-in-hand, into the maze, their hands swinging back and forth as if they don't have a care in the world. Logan wraps his arm around me, protecting me like he promised.

In the distance, something motorized—like a weed whacker—hums, competing with the weird, ghostlike music trickling out from the maze.

"I hate you all," I say. "You guys owe me a big—"

A dark figure jumps out of the corn stalks and I scream, nearly knocking down Logan in my haste to get away from the guy. He chuckles and my face burns as I step back, dusting myself off even though we didn't fall down.

Allie turns around, grinning at me.

Logan leans in to whisper in my ear, "You're fine. It's all fake."

I nod, and we follow Allie and Adam into the maze as the masked guy slinks back into the shadows, waiting for his next victim.

I walk close to Logan, nearly stepping on his toes. I lean in, whispering into his ear, "I knew we shouldn't have come. I've made it thirty seconds and I think I might pee my pants."

"Wet blanket, wet blanket, wet blanket," Allie singsongs, skipping ahead down the path, her hand in Adam's. I ignore the way Logan's looking at me.

I've never told Allie that it bothers me, how she views me like some sort of buzzkill, because I'd have to tell her *why* it bothers me. I'd have to admit that ever since my mom died, I view all this stuff—horseback riding, flying, public speaking—as unnecessary risks.

If my mom hadn't been such a daredevil, she'd still be alive. And my dad wouldn't look so sad all the time.

I glance up, watching as Allie merrily walks further into the maze. I don't tell her because I'm worried if I do, she still won't understand. She's the girl who will try anything and I'm the girl forever tethered to her fears.

Up ahead a series of scarecrows perch on wooden posts. Allie pushes Adam to one side of the pathway so that they won't run into them.

"Are those real people?" she whispers, not letting her eyes off them.

I share a look with Logan, and he nods toward Allie, encouraging me to step forward. I rake in a shaky breath and then let go of my death grip on his hand, stepping up beside Allie, squinting as I stare into the darkness where eyes should be. Is it a bulky mask or are there no eyes at all? "I can't tell," I say, studying them. They're the right size, but they're sitting so perfectly still, it's impossible to discern if they're stuffed or human. There's straw sticking out from their sleeves and pants and even from under their matching hats.

We're so busy staring at them that we don't notice the crowd of ghouls slinking up behind us until six pairs of hands shoot out. They swipe around, and Allie leaps forward, letting go of Adam's hand as she whirls around, so that she's standing with her back to the scarecrows. Eyes wide, she stares into the cornstalks to where the ghouls fled. "That was so not cool," she says, her voice wavering.

I stifle a laugh, sharing a smile with Logan. Allie so rarely gets scared in this place; it's nice to see her looking a little freaked for one shining moment.

Allie is still shivering ever so slightly when something moves behind her, and I watch as a scarecrow lets go of the wooden cross, dropping silently down without her noticing.

I open my mouth to warn her, but the scarecrow puts a finger to his lips, and against all logic, I snap my mouth shut. I want to tell her—some part of me is screaming at her—but I just stand there frozen as he creeps forward, and then, very slowly, extends one finger and gently touches her shoulder.

She screams at the top of her lungs and leaps forward, crashing straight into Adam's chest.

He's trying really hard not to laugh as he wraps his arms around her. Allie turns around to see the scarecrow, and then *she* laughs too. Logan wraps his arms around me from behind, and I can feel him smiling against me as he nestles his lips against my neck.

For a moment, I forget we're in this maze, the sprinkling raindrops returning as I lose myself in his touch.

Having determined that there's nothing to be afraid of, Adam and Allie begin scampering down the path again, and I pull just far enough away from Logan to walk without us tripping over each other. The path narrows, and there's no way to walk side by side, so Logan slips behind me, releasing my hand.

And then there's a weird black tunnel ahead. Screams drift out with the fake smoke.

I stop. "Oh hell no, I am not walking into there."

"Come on Harper, buck up," Adam says, smiling at me over his shoulder.

Maybe it's that simple to him, but I can't silence my fears so easily. They whisper through my veins. I take in a long, shaky breath and follow him and Allie forward, to the black structure. I see they've put strips of plastic at the door, so that once you pass through, they slip shut behind you, swallowing you up like the mouth of something ferocious. Allie steps behind

Adam, her hands on his waist, and I put my hands on Allie's shoulders. Behind me, Logan grabs my hips. And we enter the pitch-black like that, linked together in a row.

I know it's a tunnel, but it may as well be a mineshaft a thousand feet below the earth. I see nothing—no glow of the moon, no shadows, nothing but black. I would wave my hand in front of my face—just to test whether I can actually see it—but I'm afraid to let go of Allie.

A shuffling noise raises the hairs on my neck, and Logan's hands tighten on my hips. "Don't worry, I've got you," he whispers, his voice steady.

I blink, but I still can't see three inches in front of my face. All I have is my hearing to rely on, and the hope that Adam is leading us toward the end of this. Can he see any light? Does he even know where he's going?

And then I feel someone's breath, hot on my ear, and somehow I know it's not Logan. I duck away as the person—it's a him—whispers something, so low and guttural that I can't make it out. A chill winds its way down my spine. I lose my grip on Allie and find Logan's hand in the darkness, pulling him along toward a faint yellow glow in the distance. I trip on something and he barely holds me up.

And then we stumble out of the darkness, and the moon seems unreasonably bright in comparison. I blink.

Allie's a little pale, now, but Adam is grinning.

"Did someone whisper in your ear? God that was creepy," Adam says.

I laugh, masking the shakiness I feel. "Uh, yeah." I roll my shoulders, trying to loosen up the tightness in my neck and back.

Luckily, the path has widened again. We step forward, deeper into the maze, when a giant black creature drops in front of Allie.

She screams, an ear-splitting scream, and jumps backward, knocking me down into the gravel at the exit to the tent.

It's a giant rubber spider. I look up and can just make out the pole supporting it extending out over the tent exit. We *totally* should have seen it coming.

I laugh. "Okay, that was stupid."

Allie stands and helps me to my feet. I wipe the dust off my jeans and we set out again, surrounded by the eerie music being piped in from somewhere.

And then we emerge from the corn maze, and relief floods through me. That was quick. I made it.

But then I see the cones, guiding us across a short open field and to a second corn patch, and I realize that the pain isn't over yet. We set out across the expanse, and for a moment, I'm just happy that we're back in open space. No one whispering in my ear, no one dropping giant spiders on our heads. I relax a little bit, taking a deep breath, as the sprinkling of raindrops thickens to a steady drizzle.

Logan frowns and looks up, opening his mouth as if he's about to speak. But then an engine screams out into the silence. I whirl around to see a man in a white mask standing at the edge of the first cornfield, staring straight at me with dark, hollow eyes. He revs a chainsaw and we all freeze, stare back.

And then he bursts into a dead run, glaring right at us, his chainsaw roaring into the night air.

"Holy—"

We take off, racing for the security of the cornstalks. I skid across a slippery spot of grass, and Logan's at my elbow, catching me before I fall. The chainsaw guy gets closer, but we're at the entrance to the second maze now. We flood into it.

The maze forks to the left, and I race in that direction, turning right and left again, until the sounds of the chainsaw drift away, and the maze falls silent. I slow to a walk, panting for breath and turn to speak to Logan—to beg him to just *leave* with me, but he's not there. My stomach plunges. No one is. I'm alone, surrounded by nothing but seven-foot-tall cornstalks. I stop and twist around, trying to figure out where Logan went, just as the sky really lets loose, rain drops darkening the ground around me.

I'm cold suddenly, acutely aware of the way the shadows bend and move with the breeze, the cornstalks rustling. Above, dark clouds build, blotting out the stars and the moon. A shiver rolls down my spine.

I force myself to focus. My friends must have gone right at the entrance to the maze. I blink, fear tightening in my chest as I twist around, desperate for them to appear, to round a corner.

I don't want to be alone in here.

Something rustles behind me and I turn around, praying it's Logan.

It's not.

49

A man in a gruesome mask steps out. The mask makes it look like his face is melting off, showing off pieces of his skull.

I step backward as he inches closer to me, and we maintain just a dozen feet between us. As I step back again, fear coiling in my stomach, my heel catches on an uneven spot in the path, and I go down, slamming into my elbows.

He chooses that moment to lunge at me. I scramble backward on my hands, like a crab, and then whirl around and bolt, slamming right into another body.

I try to scream, but it comes out as a whimper as someone's arms tighten around me.

"Shhhh." The word is breathy, hot in my ear, distinctively male. He hugs me tighter. *"Shhhh,"* comes the gravelly voice again. "It's okay."

The panic vanishes and I melt into Logan, the relief so swift my knees almost buckle. He came back for me.

"Sorry. I just got freaked out. That guy—" I turn and my voice cuts off as I realize he's gone, that he's slipped back into the cornstalks to wait for his next victim.

"What guy?" he says, as the rain comes down harder. He glances up at the sky, blinking as a drop lands on his nose. His jaw clenches as he shakes his head.

"Um, nothing." The sounds of the rain heighten, the drops hitting the leaves around us.

"Crap," Logan says, looking up at the darkened clouds once more. "I just realized I left a bunch of my uncle's tools on the back deck. *Power* tools. They're probably ruined already."

"Oh, that sucks." I turn to him, taking in his damp, nearly jet-black hair. He furrows his brow as the rain slides down his face.

"Yeah. Maybe I can still get them. Can you get a ride home with Adam?" He steps forward, kissing me so quickly I barely have the chance to kiss him back before he steps away. "I'll call you, okay?"

And then he jogs off, back the way he came. A bolt of lightning flashes as he disappears around the corner.

"Are you trying to get struck by lightning?" Allie's voice calls out. I turn to see her standing at the bend of the maze, her hood pulled up over her face. "Where's Logan?"

I swallow and plaster a smile on my face. "He had to go. Let's finish the maze and get out of here before the storm gets worse."

I follow them into the last section of the maze. *It's all going to be okay*, I tell myself. But then a car alarm goes off in the distance and I run.

CHAPTER FIVE

Adam drops me off near the back door of my house, and I dash out of his truck as the rain pounds down around me. He waits until I'm inside, honks twice, and tears out of the driveway.

Inside the empty house, the sound of the rain is a steady hum, the drops streaming down the old aluminum windows, obscuring the view of the drenched pastures. A yellow glow emanates from the barns, where I know I'd find my dad if I suddenly got the urge to look for him.

I hang my dripping jacket up near the door, then kick off my saturated cowboy boots and peel off my wet socks before going to the fridge to grab a soda. As I take the first sip, I reach into my pocket to check my phone for messages.

But there's nothing in my pocket. Not my phone. Not my wallet. Nada. I walk back to my jacket and strike out again—there's nothing there but my car key.

My phone is in my purse.

Which is in Logan's Jeep.

I sigh. If it were Sunday, I'd just wait one day and get my stuff from Logan at school. But it's Friday and I don't want to go all weekend without my things.

I stare at the house phone, trying to remember Logan's phone number. But I can't even come up with the first digit. It's programmed into my cell, so I doubt I've ever dialed it.

I've never been to Logan's house, but I know where he lives. All he had to do was describe the place, and I knew exactly which house he meant—the one that used to belong to the Carsons. Apparently, the whole place is a wreck—Logan's helping his uncle fix it up—so that's why he's never invited me over.

But I don't think he'd be upset if I just showed up. I need my stuff. I go to the back door and slip back into my jacket, then find a pair of rubber boots from the pile on the back porch, not bothering with socks. I'll only be gone a minute. I dash across the patio, my head ducked to keep the rain out of my eyes. I fling myself into the front seat of the battered old Honda Civic my dad got for five hundred bucks when I turned sixteen. I yank the door shut just as another bolt of lightning flashes, followed by the growing rumble of thunder.

I start my car and head toward Logan's house, carefully navigating the twisting, winding country roads, past old farms and sprawling pastures, until I'm at the edge of town.

As I round the final curve, overgrown bushes line the street, obscuring a black iron fence. Logan's uncle's Suburban—I've seen it once before, when we ran into his uncle in town—is just pulling out of the driveway as it comes into view, but he goes the opposite direction.

Just as he disappears around the curve, I pull to a stop between two giant pillars, each of which is topped by a sandstone lion, its mouth open in an eternal roar, exposing white stone teeth. I stare up at them through the rain streaming down my windows, before turning back to the path in front of me. To my right, an old black mailbox sits, the door cracked open.

I wonder if Logan has ever received bloody cow bones in that mailbox. I guess he would have said something if he had.

I blink away the image of blood and bones, and drive between the two black iron gates hanging crookedly on broken hinges. I glide down the splintered concrete driveway, my tires squashing the grass sprouting between the cracks.

When I reach the front of the old Victorian mansion, one of the founding homes in Enumclaw, I stop and put my coupe into park.

As I look up at the house, all the spooky stories we used to tell each other as kids come back to me. Supposedly, the estate was built in the late 1890s for the Carson family. They lived there—here—for three generations, until they all died on a dark, stormy night back in the sixties. A married couple, their three kids, and the grandmother. All found dead, all killed in different ways. They think the dad did it, but the cops were never totally convinced. It was too bizarre. Too . . . twisted.

Goosebumps rise along my arms. The house probably looked just like this that night, with its rain-slicked roof, lightning flashing.

I take a deep breath, attempting to quell my nerves.

Ever since the original family's death, the mansion has changed hands over and over again until it finally started falling into disrepair. The house is beautiful and gothic, but it began showing its age years ago. Now, the paint is peeling and the grass is too long and some of the windows are covered by dark sheets, most likely to mask cracks or stop drafts.

I glance back at the way I came. The wooded entry feels even narrower, as if the trees threaten to close up and block anyone who wants to come in—or go out.

Fifty years ago, before their tragic end, the original owners started a Christmas tree farm. After they died, the farm quit selling trees, but the trees didn't quit growing. They now form a thick forest, blocking the home's view of the Green River valley. People say that you could once see the house from the road. But you can't anymore. The dark shadows block it from view.

I guess that's part of the spookiness of it. It's hidden back here, behind fifty-year-old fir trees, just a hundred yards from the cliffside. When we were kids, it was "that house"—the one you'd dare your friends to run up to and touch. No one ever did, though. No one had the guts.

I can hardly make out the house through the raindrops snaking down my windshield, so I kill the engine and climb out, rushing across the lawn to the front porch. The old wooden steps creak as I bound up them.

Under the cover of the porch, I twist around and stare back the way I came, listening as the rain pounds the roof, spills from the overflowing gutters. Lightning streaks across the sky, and almost immediately, the thunder rumbles, building and growing until it's like I can feel it beneath my feet.

I turn back to the door and knock, then wait, wondering belatedly if I look like a drowned rat.

No one answers. I glance back and confirm Logan's Jeep is parked next to my beat-up car, and then knock again, this time louder. Just as my fist connects for the third time, the door creaks open.

Logan's standing in front of me. He looks different than he did just an hour ago—more athletic? And yet somehow less relaxed. He's changed out of his jeans and sweater and into loose-fitting track pants and a long-sleeved T-shirt with an Adidas logo, a matching ball cap slung low over his eyes, making them look darker.

His whole outfit reminds me of the soccer-ball shifter I noticed today in his Jeep.

"Um, hey," I say, suddenly nervous. He left so soon after me freaking out and, weirdly, I feel like I shouldn't be here.

His grin is foreign, more like the Cheshire Cat than his normal warm smile as he steps aside so that I can come into the house. I walk into the large foyer, and he shoves the door shut behind me, twisting the lock. The sound of the bolt slamming shut echoes down the empty hall.

The rain is nearly as loud inside as it is out.

I turn to Logan. "I left my purse in your car," I say, running a hand through my damp hair. "It has my cell, or I would have called you first."

56

He gives me a blank, totally unreadable look. "I know. It's in the kitchen."

"Oh. Good," I say, feeling stupid. Maybe it's because he's still standing a few feet away, not closing the distance to kiss me like he usually does when we see each other. But I don't think that's totally it either. Something about my being here seems wrong, off. I try to push it from my mind. "Sorry for bugging you. I just need to get it back, and then I'll head home."

"Sure, Harper. Hang up your coat and come in."

There's something weird about the way he says my name, too. Like he's trying it out for the first time.

"Should I take off my boots?" I ask, looking down at his socks.

"Sure." He shrugs, and I feel awkward again. He should be smiling at me. Hugging me. Does he think I overreacted at the maze when that creepy masked guy came after me?

I kick off my rubber boots and follow him, wondering if maybe my over-the-top freak-out is what really sent him home in such a rush, and the tools were a ruse. My bare feet are silent on the worn, cold hardwood. There are dark inlaid diamond shapes in the floor every few feet, and then the narrow hall opens up into an enormous kitchen. My purse lies on the tiled countertop, which looks like it was redone—poorly—in the eighties.

He grabs it and tosses it at me, and I barely manage to catch it. "Did you want a tour, *Harper*?"

I blink. He *is* saying my name weirdly, right? It's not all in my head? Maybe I'm just being paranoid.

"Oh. Um, yeah, sure." I glance around, taking in the toolbox on the table and the sheets of plywood stacked up in the empty living room. They really have been working on this place.

"Great. Let's start upstairs."

He walks past me, and I impulsively reach for him, intertwining my fingers with his. He hesitates a second, glancing down at my hand, before he pulls me toward the stairway, and finally, I get the smile, the warmth of recognition. It transforms his face.

So maybe he *had* been worried. Only not about what I thought. Did he think I was angry with him for bailing so abruptly? That would explain his hesitance.

We walk up the hardwood stairs, following a burgundy-and-blue oriental runner up to a landing where rain streams down a stained-glass window. My left hand glides over the banister as we climb the second half of the stairs and Logan pulls me against him. I unwind a little, glad that weird distance between us is gone.

"My house was too quiet when I got home," I say.

He glances back at me. "Yeah?"

"Totally. It's not the same without you."

Understatement of the year. In the dead silence of my house, all I do is think about Logan.

We make it up the stairs, where three dark wooden doors sit closed. "That's my uncle's room," he says, pointing to the door at the end of the hall. "This one is mine."

He twists the old crystal doorknob and we step inside. "I've only lived here a few months, so I haven't really put up much stuff," he says, slipping his hand from mine and crossing the room to look out the window.

The dim light from the fixture mounted at the peak of the roof, just outside the window, reflects oddly through the glass. It makes the shadows of the raindrops appear to be sliding down Logan's face, making it impossible to read his expression through the dark angles and shadows.

I stand in the doorway, taking in the heavy antique furniture. A queen-sized bed with a thick red quilt takes up one wall, the headboard and footboard sporting enormous, twisted cordials. Opposite is a battered teak five-drawer dresser, one brass handle missing from the second drawer.

Thick, dark blue drapes adorn each of the two windows.

"It's probably not what you expected, but I like it."

When he turns away from the window, he stares into my eyes so intently it's like a challenge. Like he just *wants* me to say that I don't like it.

I nod, tearing my gaze away from him. I must just be creeped out by the maze and the raging storm, or maybe it's the memory of the dead birds and the cow bones. I'm reading between the lines, seeing things that aren't there.

I don't say anything in response. The truth is, I do like the room. I mean, yeah, it's not what I pictured for Logan, but it's oozing with elegance and old world charm. I wonder if the furniture was picked out from antique shops and flea markets, or if it's been here for decades.

"Anyway, the basement is where the cool stuff is. Come on."

Logan puts his arm loosely around my waist, but there's an awkwardness to it as he guides me down the stairs, back to the foyer. Then we turn to a five-paneled, white-painted door with an antique knob like the one on Logan's room.

The door sticks, but he yanks hard and it squeaks open. He reaches in and pulls at a string hanging from the ceiling. A single lightbulb flickers to life, illuminating the narrow wooden stairs. It swings back and forth on the wire, making the shadows on the walls sway and bend.

"Ladies first," he says, holding the door open.

I take a tentative step onto the dusty, decaying steps and immediately regret having removed my shoes when I entered the house.

"Don't worry," Logan calls out. "Nothing here bites."

"You sure about that?" I say, gripping hold of the worn wooden railing as I slowly begin my descent.

Logan steps onto the staircase behind me, and it creaks under his weight. "Basements . . . do they scare you?"

I breathe deeply through my mouth, trying to avoid the musty, dank scent. "They're not on my list or anything. But they still creep me out when they're so dark and musty."

"Well . . ." Logan says as we set foot on the basement floor, "let's see if we can't get you some more light." He pulls on another string, and then another, and the room immediately brightens. But somehow the light makes the space even less inviting. The cinder-block walls sport dark spots—possibly from the rain. The floor is bare cement, and boxes are stacked all over the place, from corner to corner. The ceiling is covered in cobwebs and too low for comfort. There are no windows to be found.

"Uh, this is the cool part why, exactly?"

Logan chuckles. "I know, it's kind of creepy at first. But this house is a hundred and twenty years old, so you have to look beyond the aesthetics."

I nod. "And what exactly would I be seeing if I looked beyond that?"

"The boxes."

I snort.

"I'm serious, *Harper*. Most of them aren't that old, but a few are pretty amazing. I think they were left behind in the sixties, when the original family died. By the looks of the boxes, no one's bothered with them in years. The dust on them must have been an inch thick. My uncle hasn't set foot down here since he bought the place last summer."

"But you have," I say.

He nods. "Oh yeah, I spend a lot of time down here," he says, his tone eager. He moves to a wall of boxes, pulling his hat off and running a hand through his shaggy hair. When his dark hair moves, I catch a glimpse of a scar behind his temple just before he puts the hat back on his head. I want to ask him where he got the scar, but he opens his mouth to explain something, so I decide not to pry.

"I started on this wall over here, but it's mostly household stuff. Tablecloths, sheets, that sort of thing."

"Mm-hmm. I know you wanted to give me the grand tour and everything, but I really don't think some tablecloths are enough to make me like this place." I cross my arms, hoping it'll shield the sound of my quickening heartbeat.

"Oh, don't worry. You will." Logan winks.

"And how's that?" I raise my eyebrows.

"I'm glad you asked." He pauses. And then with a flourish of his arm, he says, "This wall, over here, this is the good stuff."

Reluctantly, I cross the space, my toes growing cold. I'm halfway there when the light-bulbs dim, then grow bright, then dim again.

Logan glances up at the dangling lights. "Sorry about that. The house has a bit of an electrical issue down here. Especially during thunderstorms like this."

I swallow. "Are you sure we should be down here?"

He waves a hand over his shoulder, too busy looking through a box to see what must be a freaked-out expression on my face. "Nah, we're fine. The lights usually stay on."

Usually. That's comforting.

"Ah! Here it is!" He produces a leather-bound photo album.

"And what is *it*, exactly?" I ask, stepping up beside him.

"The Carson family photo album." He pushes it toward me. "Seriously. Take a look." Then he motions to a stool sitting close to the boxes. "Your chair, madam."

I nod and take a seat as I pull the album onto my lap. The spine cracks as I flip it open.

A woman with an apron and a glowing smile beams up at me. Dark curls frame her face.

"That's the one they found hanging from the banister."

62

I snap the book shut and look at my hand. My left hand. The hand I slid along the banister just moments ago when we trailed down the stairs. My skin must have touched the spot where that dead woman tied the rope.

Logan chuckles. "I thought you said you knew all the stories," he says, looking up from the box he's digging through. In the dim light of the bare bulbs, his eyes have an odd, shadowed look to them, making them look more black than brown.

My heart climbs into my throat. "I did. They're like urban legends at school. But it's different seeing a personal family photo album while sitting in the basement of their house."

A chill sweeps down my spine.

"Still. This is history we're talking about. Flip to the third page."

I swallow, slide my fingers over the cover, and find the third page, where twin little girls in matching polka-dotted jumpers stare back at me, sitting side by side on identical bicycles with cute little baskets.

"The twins were six. They say he drowned them in the bathtub."

I snap the book shut again and stand, the stool clattering to the floor behind me.

"Just stop it," I hiss, shoving the photo album into the nearest box.

"Stop what?" he asks, his hands buried in a box. "Ah, I found it." He pulls out a rusted metal hook. "You know what this is?"

"It's a hay hook," I snap. I'm not amused by whatever game

he's playing. Is this because I freaked out at the maze? "We have them at my house for feeding the cows. Makes it easier to pull hay bales."

"It *was* a hay hook," he says, excited now. "But they say he used it to drag the bodies—"

"Logan!" I yell. "Just sto—"

And then the lights go out, and my stomach plunges to my knees. His stories, the shadows in his eyes, the pictures of the little girls, just six years old. It's too much. Now that Logan's silent, and the lights are out, I can make out the sound of the rain pounding the earth on the other side of the basement walls.

"I want out of here," I say, my voice pathetic and gargled thanks to the lump in my throat. I'm afraid to move it's so dark.

I hear something—Logan or mice, I don't want to know. But then I feel his breath, hot on my ear. "Stop it," I say, panic rising as I whirl around to face him. Or where I think he is. It's pitch-black down here. I step back, a tiny, tentative step, my bare heel connecting with something. The stool?

I turn in the direction I hope will lead me to the stairs and tiptoe forward, my toes sliding across the concrete. I blink, again and again, willing my eyes to adjust to the darkness. I just want to see. Something. Anything that would tell me where he is, where I am, how to get out of here. "Logan?" I say. "Where'd you go?"

He's silent.

"Stop screwing around. I'm freaked the hell out, okay? I

hope you're happy." I purse my eyes shut and then open them again, but it's pitch-black either way.

He doesn't speak. I creep forward another step, and then I feel something cold against the back of my neck.

Cool, curved metal. In an instant, I know what it is, know he's sliding the back of the hook along my skin.

And then my shirt is tightening around my throat, and he's pulling me back. My heart explodes in my throat. "This isn't funny!" I say, my voice strangled. I twist around and my shirt tears, breaks free, and then I lunge toward the steps as Logan laughs.

My vision is still nothing but inky black, and I don't know how close I am to the stairs until I trip on them. I hit the bottom step with my toes and fall down, hard, my shins and knees hitting the steps just as the lights come back on.

I twist around so that I'm sitting on the stairs staring back at Logan as my eyes swim with tears. He's doubled over, laughing, still holding the hook in one hand.

"What the hell is wrong with you?" I ask, my voice trembling as tears stream down my cheeks. I sniffle, frantically wiping away the tears, willing myself under control as my lip trembles. "You're an asshole. Stay away from me." And then I turn and scramble up the steps, on my hands and feet until I get to the top.

The door sticks again and I shove so hard I tumble to the floor.

Logan laughs louder, and the sound of it rings in my ears as I flee the house.

CHAPTER SIX

On Monday, I step out of my car in the gravel lot at school, pulling my hood over my hair. I glance down at the rocks beneath my feet, just to make sure there are no birds, no feathers, no blood. I don't think I could handle that today.

The rain that pounded all weekend has finally let up, lessening to little more than a drizzle. I cross the lot and round the building, pushing my way through a steel door and into the bright light of the gym.

Two long tables are set up along one side, where a group of girls are unrolling butcher paper and squirting paint into little bowls. Madison stands with a clipboard in one hand, and a handful of paintbrushes in the other, ever the mistress of the situation. It's no wonder they're letting her manage the whole event.

I turn away from her and scan the room for Allie until I find her sitting cross-legged on the floor, dipping a paintbrush into a cup of paint.

I wanted to back out on the stupid Halloween Masquerade decorations—if only because helping Madison on *anything* is totally against my principles—but I promised Allie I'd help, and besides, I really need to talk to her. She was at her out-of-town race with her parents all weekend and I really need her to tell me what the heck I'm supposed to say to Logan, because I have to see him in a half hour when first period starts.

I shrug away a chill as I think of the darkness in his eyes, remember the sound of his cackling, cruel laughter. Remember the dead silence when the lights went out, and he crept up behind me.

I can't get over how shocking his behavior was on Friday. How positively gleeful he was over terrorizing me.

I walk up to Allie, where she's laying half-across an enormous stretch of butcher paper, staring down at a rather lopsided witch's hat, her lips screwed up to the side. When she looks up at me, her frown transforms into a smile. "Oh good! You're here!" She motions to the wet paint. "This whole thing looks ridiculous. *Help!*"

"I don't know how great I'm going to be at doing this, but okay . . ." I sink to the floor and sit cross-legged, watching as she tries to even out the two sides of the hat. I'm not really sure what the mural is going to become, but so far she's got a frog, a broomstick, and some kind of cape. Leave it to Allie to worry about the clothes and accessories before the actual witch.

She glances up at me as she works. "How was your weekend?"

I pick up a bat-shaped sponge and dip it in some paint, chewing on my lip. "Uh, not good."

"Why not?"

"I'm not really sure if I'm *with* Logan anymore."

"What?" She jerks her hand just as she's dipping the brush into the paint, and the whole cup tips over. "Crap." She grabs at some paper towels, mopping up the mess from the linoleum floor. I grab a few extra and begin cleaning up alongside her.

Naturally, that's when the door to the gym opens. I look up to see Logan stride through, my heart dropping to my stomach.

"Great." I consider making a mad dash for the exit, but we share first period anyway, so it's not like I'm going to be able to avoid him all day.

Instead, I just sit there, glued to my spot, watching him walk up. Oddly enough, he doesn't have the look of someone who just scared his girlfriend out of her mind. His smile is tentative and, if anything, he seems concerned. I continue evaluating his expression when suddenly he speaks. "Hey. I dropped by to pick you up like usual, but you weren't home." He looks down at the mural. "You want a hand with this stuff?"

I stare at him. "You really think I want your help right now?"

He eyes me quizzically and reaches for a cup of red paint.

"Thanks. We got it." I pull the cup of paint a few inches from his reach.

He picks it up again, and this time I yank it away so hard it splashes over the rim, onto my hand. "I said we got it."

Logan narrows his eyes at me. "I thought maybe you didn't

answer my texts yesterday because you were busy. But you're actually mad at me, aren't you?"

"Ya think?" I glare back at him, ignoring the paint running down my hand. It drips onto the butcher paper.

"Look, I'm really sorry I had to leave early from the maze—"

"The maze? You think I'm upset about the maze?" I rub the back of my paint-covered hand against the butcher paper, glancing at the speckles that have already begun to dry. They look like drops of blood.

Logan's brow wrinkles in confusion. "Umm . . . I'm sorry, but I guess I must have missed something." He slides his hands into his pockets. "What else do you have to be upset about?"

I slam the mostly empty cup of paint against the paper. "How about how you were a total asshole at your house?"

Logan visibly recoils. "You came to my house?"

"Don't play stupid with me, Logan. You scared the crap out of me and then laughed about it. And you ripped my favorite shirt."

He pales. "I didn't hurt you, did I?"

"Why do you care? You seemed to think it was funny as hell at the time." I shiver just thinking about the way he rubbed the hook against my skin.

"Harper—"

"Just leave me alone," I say, through gritted teeth. Allie's staring at me like I've grown a second head.

"But—"

"*Leave*." I say again, glaring at him, hard.

He looks like he wants to say more, but he's at a loss, which is just fine with me.

Madison walks up and for once I'm relieved to see her. "Hey, Logan. Did you come to help with the decorations? Because I really need someone *strong* to work on the custom table we're designing." She reaches for his arm, giving his bicep a suggestive squeeze while smiling demurely. "It's going to hold a bunch of dry ice so it will make fog clouds all night."

She couldn't lay it on thicker if she had a spatula.

Logan doesn't even look at her.

"He would *love* to help you," I say, when he doesn't turn away.

Logan glances over at Madison, finally allowing her to drag him across the room and out of earshot, but not without glancing back at me a half-dozen times.

"Um, wow. Intense!" Allie says, "What was that about?"

"You know, I actually don't want to talk about it anymore," I say, staring at the mural to avoid her eyes.

"You sure?" She looks up from her paint cup, studying my face.

"Yeah. I'll tell you all about it later. Let's just paint this mural."

"Ooooookaaay," she says, unconvinced.

"Thanks. I appreciate it."

I wipe the remaining crimson paint off my hand and then set to work, adding beady little eyes to the bats.

They're as black as Logan's eyes had been just before the lights cut off in the basement.

• • •

I wait until the last minute to walk through the classroom door and am not surprised to discover that Logan's already sitting there, sunk down in his chair, staring at his binder. When he sees me, he sits up straighter and watches me walk toward him.

It takes everything I have to ignore his gaze. I walk right past him and sit down just as Mr. Patricks begins handing out a stack of papers to the first student in each of the rows.

"Okay, guys. We're going to have time to outline our campaigns today, so look over this list and then assemble in your groups. I expect a basic overview of your plans by the end of class."

Great. I'd take a pop quiz over group time with Logan. I'm just going to hear that terrible, cackling laugh of his—the one that I never knew he had—over and over as I imagine the cold steel of the rusty hook gliding across my skin.

The last paper lands on my desk, and I stare down at it, the words blurring together. Just as the first chairs screech on the tile floors, I shoot out of my seat, walking straight to Mr. Patricks.

"May I use the hall pass?"

He nods and waves at the big wooden GIRLS pass hanging by the door. I slip it from the hook and step into the hall, taking in a big gulp of air.

How am I supposed to sit next to Logan all day, all week, all year? I really thought we had something special, but after what happened on Friday . . .

I slip into the girls' bathroom around the corner and then

lean against the cold cinder-block wall, my eyes closed, taking in deep breaths. It hurts to be so close to him. Hurts to think of the way he smiled at me, kissed me, held me.

It hurts because I want him so much, despite the way he treated me at his house.

The door creaks and I open my eyes just in time to see Logan step in.

"This is the girls' bathroom," I say, stepping away from the wall.

"I know, but I have to talk to you."

"I don't want to talk."

As he stands in front of me, it's hard to reconcile this guy and the one who laughed at me at his house. He's defeated. Like he knows he's lost no matter what happens next. "There's something you need to know, Harper. You can still hate me but you deserve to know."

I walk to the bathroom sink and wash my hands, ignoring his reflection behind me. The last time I stood in here, I was trying to forget the image of those birds as he was putting a rose in my locker.

And now it's my own boyfriend I want to disappear. "I told you. I don't want to talk to you. Why can't you understand that? We're done."

"No, Harper . . . let me explain." He reaches out to touch my shoulder.

I jerk away. "I don't need your explanation. I can't believe I told you about how I have all these fears, things that I've been afraid of since my mother died, and you bring me down to your unbelievably creepy basement and taunt me with a murdered family's mementos."

Logan pales. "It wasn't me."

"I'm not an idiot. Of course it was you."

"I have a twin brother," he says all in one breath, the words landing on top of one another.

They ring in my ears as I go still, my hands under the running water. I look up at him in the mirror, taking in the light reflecting in his eyes, the stiffness in his shoulders. "No you don't."

He meets my eyes in the mirror. They look so different than they did on Friday. They're a warm chocolate shade, filled with such strong emotion it's hard to imagine him as the cruel boy from the basement, eyes as dark as the storm clouds outside his house. "Yes, I do," he says, his voice strangled, *wrong*. Like it's hard to say the words.

I shake my head, my hair slipping into my eyes. "Then why haven't I seen him at school?"

His shoulders deflate. "Daemon was expelled from Cedar Cove. We all decided it would be better for him if he were homeschooled."

Daemon. A name he's never spoken. How could he have kept this hidden from me? I swallow. "What did he do?"

"Will you just face me, please?" He wraps his hand around my shoulder, and I turn away from him, away from the sink. We're only a foot apart as I look up, take in the pain in his eyes. I could get lost in them . . . in it. He swallows. "A lot of things. We might look alike, but . . . we're completely different people.

He's not a very nice person. He's angry all the time, and bitter. I never wanted you to meet him. I didn't think you needed to."

I can't believe this. I can't believe he'd lie to me this way. Not just once, but over and over and over again.

"So it was him at your house?"

He nods. "Yeah. God, I am so sorry. I know what he's like, and when we first got together, I kind of talked myself into thinking you didn't need to know about him. I had no idea you'd come over on Friday. I was with my uncle, and Daemon didn't say anything to me when I got home."

"That's why you never wanted me over at your house." Anger, frustration, hurt . . . it all boils together in my stomach. "And you just thought . . . what?" I say, my voice rising, echoing off the tall ceiling. "That you'd just keep hiding it? For how long, Logan? How was that going to work?"

"I don't know," he says, his voice low and dejected. "I knew it wouldn't. But the more I cared for you, the harder it became."

"Do you even know how much he scared me on Friday? How could you lie to me like this?" I blink, my eyes stinging.

"I'm sorry." Logan falls silent again, looking away as he chews his bottom lip. "I should have told you about him before, but I was so desperate to not be defined by him, to not have people look at me with these pitying looks just because of him. Because of the trouble he causes. This was supposed to be my fresh start. And maybe you can't understand that, but I had to try."

I feel sorry for him and infuriated at the same time. For now, though, my disappointment wins out. "What am I supposed to do, Logan? Pretend you didn't lie? Be relieved that the guy in the basement wasn't my boyfriend after all?"

"I don't know. But you *deserve* the truth. And there it is. I have a twin brother and I wish you'd never met him."

I nod, in a noncommittal sort of way, still trying to process it all as I run my hands under my eyes to wipe away the tears that have managed to escape, desperate to look normal and not like I'm actually having a meltdown.

"I think that I was just so confused after my parents' deaths. You know, they were so recent—just like a year and a half ago for my dad and a couple months ago for my mom—I think I kind of felt like I didn't have any family left. But . . ." His voice trails off.

"But?"

"But that's not true. I have Daemon." There's an air of finality to Logan's voice, as if he's just reached an epiphany from which there's no going back.

I turn away from him, staring downward at the sink, ignoring his reflection in the mirror. "And your uncle?" I add.

"Yeah, and my uncle." He pauses. "Though we still haven't really connected and he's away on business a lot. That's actually one of the reasons I feel like you get me so much . . . because we're kind of in the same boat family-wise."

My heart breaks at that one. I do know how it is. I know *exactly* how it feels, to spend days and days alone, wondering if anyone would really care if you just disappeared.

He looks at me longingly, his eagerness to erase the events of Friday night visible on his face. "Can you forgive me?"

"I don't know," I say, my voice so low it's barely audible.

"Please?" he whispers. "I should have told you. I know I should have told you."

"I said I don't know." My answer comes automatically. I grip the countertop so hard my fingers ache. Then, feeling him still standing there behind me, I add, more earnestly this time, "Really, Logan, I don't."

"Fair enough."

I don't look up as he leaves the bathroom. A moment later, I shut the sink off and go back to the hall, heading toward my locker before I walk back to class. I have some face powder in there, and I want to at least apply a little to get rid of the pale and blotchy look I have from fighting away tears.

I'm spacing out a little as I do the combo, so it takes me two tries. When I finally pop it open, a long-stemmed rose swings toward me, and I barely manage to keep it from falling on the dirty hall floor.

I grab the flower, feeling melancholy about it, so different from the joy I'd felt over the first one. He must have put it in my locker this morning, before he found out what Daemon did on Friday.

I'm about to toss it into a nearby garbage can when I see the ribbon tied around the stem in a little bow, a small scrap of paper slipped underneath.

I slide it out and unfold the note.

Roses are red
Violets are blue
I bet you didn't know
I've been watching you

CHAPTER SEVEN

I gasp, feel like I'm choking on nothing, dropping the note as I cover my mouth with my hands. I glance over my shoulder, looking for someone *literally* watching me, but I'm alone in the hallway.

I turn back to my locker and start digging through the wrinkled homework and discarded candy wrappers until I find it. A note Logan and I had been passing in class just a week ago.

I smooth it out against my locker door and reach down to grab the poem. I hold it up next to the note from the rose, studying the writing.

It doesn't match. Logan's writing is upright, neat. Meanwhile, the writing on the note is slanted, darker, more scribbly. Almost as if the person who wrote it was manic.

I shove both papers into my locker and slam the door.

It's not my boyfriend leaving me the roses after all.

● ● ●

I find myself thinking about Logan and the scary note in equal measure for the rest of the day, including the half hour I spend in the library avoiding him during lunch. By the time I make it to agricultural mechanics—ag mech, my final class of the day—I'm just happy to have Bick to distract me.

I go to my cubby to fish out my rubber hairband—required for this class—and safety goggles. Also required. Also very ugly. I'm no fashionista, but even I have standards.

"Hey DQ, you done with your gate hook yet?" Bick asks as I step into the shop, his safety glasses resting crookedly on top of his head.

I swallow, dismissing the image of another hook, and fake a smile. "I got the loop done," I say, holding up a twisted chunk of metal that used to be straight. "Just not the . . . hook at the other end."

"Ah. Plenty of time."

I shrug and follow him deeper into the shop. We each grab a thick leather apron and then cross the expansive space, sparks flying through the air around us. I dodge a hammer and then glare at the kid who had tossed it to his buddy with no regard for my precious head.

There's something comforting about this class. A chance to be myself. Which is funny, really, since I'm the only girl in this class. Allie might be adventurous, but she'd never dream of taking a welding class.

For an hour every day, I hang out with Bick, and no one cares if I'm not wearing makeup.

"You okay?" Bick asks, his eyes concerned as he looks down at me. "We missed you during lunch."

I slip on a pair of leather gloves and pick up a set of tongs, using them to grip the hook as I slide it into the glowing forge, more slowly than necessary. Even through the thick leather, I can feel the heat on my hands. Then I play with the temperature, even though I know the dial's already at its proper place.

But then I'm out of ways to stall. "Eh. Sorta."

"Something wrong?"

I just stand there, a little too warm in the gloves and apron. I lean in closer to check the forge but my hook is just beginning to glow, a deep, dark red. "Apparently, Logan has a brother I didn't know about."

"Oh."

"A *twin* brother."

"*Oh*," Bick says, his blue eyes wide. They're almost comical behind his safety goggles.

"Yeah. And he's not so nice."

"What did he do exactly?" Bick asks, his expression no longer so light and goofy. His eyes sweep over me, like he's trying to actually *see* what happened. "Are you okay?"

"He decided to pretend that he was Logan on Friday night."

"Oh." His voice falls. He purses his lips and stares into the forge, his shoulders rigid. "That's not cool."

"Yeah, and he did a bunch of stuff that totally freaked me out. And since I had no idea he wasn't really my boyfriend, I spent all weekend upset about it."

"Well, that sucks." He frowns as he turns the dial on the forge. "You should have called me. Are you okay now?"

"I guess . . ." I'm surprised by Bick's offer to call him. We've been friends for years, but we almost never hang out without Allie and Adam, except in this class.

"You guess?" His eyes flicker over at me. The genuine concern I see echoed in his eyes actually comforts me.

"Yeah," I say, and in that moment I realize that I kind of am. "It just threw me for a loop when Logan sprung this twin thing on me this morning. That's why I skipped lunch—I just needed time to process it."

"Oh. That explains why he looked so miserable." Bick grabs his own set of tongs and takes his hook from the forge, moving to the anvil to pound on the red-hot metal a few times before looking up at me. "What are you going to do?"

I grab my own tong and pull my project out, holding it away from my body as the disconfigured steel glows hot. I hold it carefully with the tong as I pick up the hammer and hit it several times, watching the metal bend around the curved tip of the anvil. When the red-hot glow cools to a burgundy shade, I go back to the forge and toss it in. "I don't know."

Bick tosses his hook back on top of mine and then turns to me. "Do you want me to talk to him?"

I shrug. "I mean, I don't even know what you'd say."

Bick steps closer, shoving his safety goggles up on his head. "I can tell him to find a new lunch table for starters."

I stare into the forge, my face growing warm, both from the heat of it and from embarrassment. I'm not the sort of girl who is used to being rescued. "No, it's fine. I have to talk to him sooner or later."

We work for a bit in silence, hammering away, putting our hooks back into the forge, hammering again.

"You gonna forgive him?" Bick asks, a few minutes later.

I stare into the heat of the forge, unblinking. "I think so."

"Really?"

I cross my arms and turn around to face him. "Yeah. I've been thinking about it all day, and I guess I get it. Why he didn't tell me about Daemon. I mean, I met the guy. I don't think I'd claim him as my brother either."

"Fair enough." Bick nods, but his eyes are somewhere else, like he's lost on another planet. He drops his hook into a bucket of water, and it hisses as it sinks to the bottom. He shuts off the forge as I drop my own hook into the bucket, and then we cross the room and hang up our leather aprons and gloves.

The final bell of the day rings, and the relief is swift. It's been such a long, up-and-down sort of day. We step through the roll-up shop door and head to the gravel parking lot where all the juniors park, taking the back sidewalks, a shortcut. It still drizzles, but it's nothing like the storm of last weekend.

I'm looking down to adjust my backpack straps when Bick stops so abruptly I ram into his back. "Whoops," I say, stumbling to a stop. "Sorry."

Bick doesn't speak, just stares out at the lot. I follow his line of sight, freezing at the image of a bloody hand on Bick's driver's side window.

"Oh my God," I say, my hand covering my mouth. "Is that—"

"I don't know," he says.

I turn and look at the car parked next to it, and it's the same thing—a bloody handprint on the driver's side glass. I spin around and take in the other cars nearby.

It's all the same. Up and down the sidewalk, students stop, stare at their cars, murmur to one another. A few students are already pulling out of the lot despite the red handprints that obscure their faces.

"This stupid parking lot is cursed," I mutter. "Birds and now bloody handprints?"

Bick and I walk slowly up to his old Toyota pickup, staring at the crimson print on the window. Bick bends down, digging through his backpack. "Maybe I have a rag or something. . . ."

I stop a foot shy of the door. The shade of red is familiar, somehow. . . .

I lean forward, until my face is inches from the glass, and take in a deep breath.

And then I stand up abruptly. "It's paint."

"How do you know?"

"It smells just like the stuff I used this morning, on the Halloween Masquerade posters. It's acrylic. Smells kinda like plastic."

I turn to the students staring at the little Corolla parked next to Bick. "It's just paint," I call out, and then turn back to look at Bick's truck again.

"But you know it was supposed to look like blood," Bick says, furrowing his brow.

"I know," I say, my throat dry. What the hell is going on in this town lately?

"What's the point?" Bick asks, shaking his head. "What exactly is the payoff here?"

I stare at the red palm on his window, at the red paint dripping down, onto the blue pickup door. "I have no idea."

"Let's go check your car," Bick says, leading me across the parking lot.

I follow him, the gravel crunching underneath my sneakers. Around me, students climb into their cars, driving away with the crimson handprints on their windows, like some kind of disturbing badge of honor.

When we get closer to my car, Bick stops, glancing between me and the window.

I stare at the handprint for a long moment. It's a darker shade of red, sort of brownish, more like brick than a fire engine. I take a deep breath and lean in to smell it, jerking back upright a moment later.

"Is it . . ."

I nod. "It doesn't smell like plastic."

The others might have been paint, but mine's different.

The handprint on my car is made of blood.

CHAPTER EIGHT

"Come on, I'll help you clean it off. We just need some wet paper towels," Bick says, motioning toward the school and its bathrooms.

I nod, feeling lost as we cross the lot again and push back into the hallways. They're nearly empty now. Where slamming lockers and bubbling voices once filled the hall, now I can hear only my footsteps.

"Maybe we should report it," Bick says, his eyes filled with concern.

I shrug. "I just want it off my car."

"Fair enough," he says, sighing. We stop at the door to the boys' bathroom. "Be right back."

Moments later he emerges, a handful of wet paper towels balled up in his fist. "Okay, come on. We'll do your car first," he announces, leading me back outside.

By the time we step outside, my battered old coupe and Bick's truck are two of the few left in the parking lot. I don't know why everyone's okay just driving off with such creepy brands on their window, but I want mine off. Now.

"Look, Mr. Richards is right there," Bick says, pointing to our principal who's currently standing on the sidewalk, talking to a few students, clipboard in hand. "Let's just tell him about your car."

I sigh. "Okay, fine. We'll tell the principal." I follow Bick across the lot, to where Mr. Richards is just stepping away from the students.

"Do you need to report your car vandalized as well?" He asks, slipping the pen behind his ear.

"Yes. But mine . . ." I swallow. "Mine isn't paint. I think it's actually blood."

He narrows his eyes, like he thinks I'm being melodramatic about some silly, insignificant prank. But then the look melts into his usual neutral, slightly smirking mask, and he nods. "Then let's go take a look."

Bick whispers to me as we cross the lot and return to my car, "I really don't think he likes teenagers."

I giggle despite myself but as we get closer to my car, my expression shifts—it's not the same. "What the heck?" I exclaim upon catching sight of the perfectly clean window. Then I turn to Mr. Richards. "I swear to you, there was a handprint on there. We just went inside to get some paper towels to clean it up."

I point to Bick and he holds up the towels. "She's right. I saw it."

Mr. Richards shrugs. "I guess it's your lucky day. The

cleaning fairy took care of it," he says, rolling his eyes. "If you'll excuse me."

He leaves us there, crosses the lot, and takes the sidewalk back to the administrative office.

"You really did see it, right?" I ask, turning to him.

Bick nods.

"The other cars had paint. I know it was blood." I swallow and look at the clean glass again.

"Yeah, I know. I saw it too." Bick reaches out, like he's going to touch my arm to make me feel better, then seems to think better of it and shoves his hands into his jacket pockets. "But you know, just because it wasn't paint doesn't mean it was real blood. It could have been the fake stuff they make at costume shops. It's almost Halloween. That stuff is probably easy to get a hold of."

I nod, not entirely convinced. If this is tied to the birds' deaths, who's to say the person couldn't get a hold of some real blood? "Yeah, whatever. I better get home, I have a million chores to do."

"Hey!" A voice calls out as I grab the handle of my car door. I turn to see Logan striding across the lot, his cheeks flushed.

"Can we catch up later?" I ask, looking up at Bick.

"Yeah. Sure. Later," Bick says, taking the hint. He walks away just as Logan reaches me.

Logan doesn't even take a breath before speaking. "Listen, I've been freaking out pretty much all day," he says. "I had no idea you even went to my house on Friday. If *he* did anything to hurt you . . ."

I stare down at the rocks, and Logan gently grabs my elbow, turning me so that he can stare straight into my eyes. "What can I do to gain your trust back? Name it. Anything you want, and I'll do it. Just give me another chance."

I open my mouth, but I don't know what to say, and I'm so swept up in the need to be close to him, in the need to just forget about dead birds and bloody handprints, that I step forward and let him slide his arms around me, let him pull me against his chest. Neither of us speaks for a long moment, and I close my eyes, remembering what it's like to feel safe in his arms.

It takes everything I have to pull myself away. "Just promise me there are no more secrets."

"I promise." Logan steps closer and tips my chin up, giving me a kiss that makes me forget about the crimson shade of blood altogether as I stand here, the world turning gray around the edges. When he steps back, he smiles in a way that tells me he's as swept away as I am. "Can we go somewhere? Dinner?"

"I can't. I have to go home," I say, frowning at the thought of the chores piling up. I'd way rather spend the evening with my boyfriend. "We can catch up tomorrow, though?"

"Oh. Okay," he says, the disappointment evident. "Yeah. See you tomorrow." I watch him walk away and then turn back, giving the glass one last look before climbing in.

I *know* it was blood on my window.

I just don't know who put it there.

Or who cleaned it off.

CHAPTER NINE

When Logan pulls into my driveway on Sunday, the autumn sun gleams on the red hood of his Jeep. The rain has finally rolled out of town, and while Logan wouldn't tell me what we were doing today, he did tell me to dress for adventure. Whatever that means. So I'm wearing hiking boots, jeans, and a pale pink sweater, hoping it's appropriate for whatever the day brings.

Logan climbs out of his car, walking around to the other side and opening the passenger door. "Your chariot awaits," he says, sweeping his arm wide.

I laugh, feeling more than a little light and giddy. Whatever rough patch we hit when I found out about Daemon has smoothed itself out.

I pause next to the door and kiss him before ducking into the car. He pushes the door shut behind me, and I buckle in as he rounds the vehicle and climbs into the driver's side.

I wait until we're out of the driveway before pestering him.

"Okay, spill."

He grins and looks over at me. "Number eight."

I freeze. "Quads?"

"Yep. We're going to Bick's house. He has a few four-wheelers."

"I know," I say, my voice as level as I can make it. "Every time we're at his house, Allie, Bick, and Adam ride, but I always just sit on the fence and watch."

"What are you worried will happen?"

"Uh . . . I'll crash."

"You won't," Logan says, half-laughing, but not in a way that makes me embarrassed.

Butterflies swarm my stomach. "I can't ride them, Logan."

He looks over at me, realizing I'm truly scared. He places a hand on my knee. "You can ride double with me until you get used to it, and then you can ride on your own. You'll be fine, I promise."

I take in a deep breath through my nose and blow it out through my mouth. "I rode them when I was little," I find myself saying. "With my mom."

Logan glances over at me but says nothing.

"I don't even remember it, but I've seen the pictures of us."

Silence fills the cab. "Is everything on your list tied to her?"

I find myself, unexpectedly, fighting tears. "Yeah. Things she's done, the person she is . . . was." My voice breaks. "I don't want to end up like her."

"How did she die?"

I blink away the tears, taking in a deep, calming breath. "She was bouldering," I say.

"Bouldering?"

I bite hard on my lip to keep it from trembling. "It's rock-climbing. With no safety ropes."

"Wow."

"Yeah. About as extreme—and as dangerous—as you can get." I blink rapidly, until I can see through the shimmering again. "She fell."

Logan squeezes my leg. "I'm sorry."

I nod, avoiding his gaze by staring out the window. "I have this whole photo album of pictures. Things she did, you know?"

"And so you made a list? From the things you saw her doing?"

I turn back to Logan. "Yes. Every one of them, she's done. The flying, the public speaking, the riding quads."

Logan stops the Jeep, even though we're nowhere near a stop sign. "You can't keep running from this. You need to get over your fears so they don't control you."

"But I'm scared." I glance behind us, relieved to see there are no cars.

"You're going to be okay. I promise, you can totally handle this."

I nod, but I'm not even remotely convinced. Visions of me flying over the handlebars swim into focus. "I'll try it once, with you. And if I hate it, you can't make me ride alone."

"Deal," he says, beaming.

I hope I don't regret this.

• • •

I stand in front of Logan with my eyes closed as he slides a lime-colored helmet over my head. I take one deep breath after another. I don't know if I can do this.

"You'll be fine," he whispers, brushing his fingertips against my chin as he buckles the strap.

I open my eyes and his reassuring smile is almost enough to calm my churning stomach. "What if I'm not? You think I can do this, but you've only known me for a month."

He steps closer, so that the visors on our helmets are touching, and puts one hand on each of my arms. "I'm not going to let anything happen to you. Just trust me."

I take in a deep breath and nod. "Okay." He stares into my eyes for a second longer, searching them. "Really. I can handle this," I say, more to myself than him.

When Logan steps out of my direct vision, I see Bick standing behind him, watching us. Waiting.

"I try for two years to get you to do this and Logan asks once and you cave," Allie calls out. I look up to see her sitting on the iron railing of the fence that surrounds the property, grinning down at me. She shoots me a thumbs-up.

Beside her, Adam smirks. "Give my poor favorite cousin a break. She's fragile."

Behind them is Bick's one-and-a-half story house, with its charming little shutters and cute little flowerbeds. I know without asking that his mom's inside, making muffins or cookies or something from scratch, and she'll show up before we're done, insisting we're all too skinny, forcing us to take a handful of treats.

I find it funny to think of Bick, in that house day after day, his mom doting all over him. He's too tough to be a mama's boy. He always rolls his eyes when she appears, but he'll still totally eat whatever she brings out.

I try to remember if my mom ever made cookies from scratch.

I look back at Bick again, but he's not meeting my gaze now. He's silent as he digs a key out of his pocket and tosses it to Logan, and we walk over to the small barn at the edge of the pasture. Bick shoves the door open, and a moment later, he rolls the first quad into the sunlight.

It's royal blue. "Cool, a Raptor," Logan says. "I had one when we lived in Cedar Cove."

Bick just grunts something unintelligible and returns to the shed for another quad. Is he mad at me for agreeing to ride for Logan's sake? Allie might give me a hard time about it, but she's not serious. What if it bugs Bick that I always told him no, and when Logan pushed, I said yes? I don't want him to be mad at me.

I blink my thoughts away, realizing Logan's still talking about Cedar Cove and riding quads up in the mountains. I'm surprised he's talking about it so simply. He doesn't mention Cedar Cove that much, and I always feel like he doesn't want to. I wonder, sometimes, if he misses it.

Logan climbs on and fires up the bike, then pats the seat, motioning for me to climb on behind him.

I take in a last ragged breath of air and then climb on, wrapping my arms tightly around his waist and resting the side of my helmet against his back. I wonder if he can hear my heart beating over the engine.

"Ready?" he calls out.

"Yeah!" I yell, but the voice inside my head screams, "Noooo!"

Logan shifts down with his foot, and then we move, slowly at first. I tighten my grip on his waist and close my eyes as the quad moves through the field. A few dozen thunderous heartbeats later, I slowly give in, peeking out through tiny slits to see the field streaming by. I sigh, and open them all the way, giving in to the inevitability of it all.

"See? This isn't so bad," Logan yells over the roar of the engine. We're not going all that fast, just sort of puttering along over the grass. There are no paths or roads, just an enormous expanse of green.

After a couple of laps around the field, I sit up a little straighter and begin to get a sense of the rhythm. Logan shifts down before corners, and we glide around them before picking up speed again in the straightaway.

Finally, he slows down by the fence line, near where Bick is sitting on a red quad, his helmet off and hanging from a handlebar. I may know nothing about quads, but I can tell his is souped up, meant to go fast. The rear wheels extend farther back and the exhaust is huge and shiny, clearly an after-market part. Allie and Adam are still sitting on the fence, cheering.

I grin as we stop, and I yank off my helmet.

I did it. I rode a quad.

"So?" Allie asks, jumping down from the fence.

"So maybe it's not quite as scary as I thought," I say.

"I told you!" Allie says, tossing her hands up in the air. "I try a million different ways to get you to ride, and in waltzes Logan, all, 'Hey, we should ride quads,' and you're all, 'Oh sure! Of course!'"

I snort. "It wasn't like that."

"Sure," Allie says winking.

Bick stands up on his quad to dig a key from his pocket, and then he tosses it at me, a gleam in his eyes. I barely manage to catch it.

Adam and Allie visibly wince.

That's when I realize we're not done yet. I'm supposed to ride by myself. The butterflies that had calmed down so nicely flap to life again.

But I can do this. I know I can.

"That's for the yellow one. It's automatic, so it should be a piece of cake," Bick says, climbing off his quad and walking toward me. "You're going to be great," he says, squeezing my shoulder.

I look over at the bike Bick's directing me to. It's just as big as the one I got off. "Are you sure?"

Adam answers for him, calling out from his place on the fence. "Definitely. A twelve-year-old can ride that quad."

Bick quietly adds, "You can go as quickly or as slowly as you like."

"And I can ride alongside you," Logan says.

"Um, okay." I nod.

Bick follows me to the yellow bike. I climb on, putting my

hands on the handlebars, fighting the urge to hold onto them with a steely death grip. "There are two brakes," he says. "This one," his hand grazes my fingers as he motions to the one on the right handlebar. "And the foot-pedal on the right. You can use either one, or both at the same time. You won't be going that fast, so it doesn't really make a difference. That's the throttle," he says, pointing to a small lever under the handle bar, near where my thumb rests.

"Got it." I glance over at Logan, who is still sitting on the other quad, waiting for me. He gives me an encouraging nod of support, his helmet bobbing. I smile at him nervously, then look back at Bick.

He meets my eyes. "You're in complete control. It'll only go as fast as you want it to. If you get scared, just let off the throttle."

I smile wider, feeling oddly relieved at his words. He said exactly what I needed to hear. I'm *in control.*

Bick hits the start button, and the bike rumbles to life beneath me. It's not as loud as the one I just got off, which is somehow reassuring. "Have fun. And be sure to slow down on those corners."

I nod. I can do this. I can totally do this. My mom may have ridden quads but it's not what killed her, or anything. It can't be *that* dangerous.

I think.

I push on the throttle with my thumb, so lightly at first that the engine just rumbles a little louder, but the quad itself doesn't move. I push harder, and the wheels finally turn, and just like that, I'm off.

My arms and legs are tense at first, as if the bike is going to take off on its own if I don't hang on tightly enough, but eventually, I feel myself relax, settle into the ride. Logan rolls along next to me, his helmet moving up and down as he glances back and forth between me and the stretch of grass in front of him.

After a full lap, my confidence grows, and I pick up speed, gliding through the fields faster and faster with each turn.

My grin spreads across my face. I wasted so much time being afraid of these things . . . and for what? They're amazing. I feel like I'm flying.

The corner looms closer, and I let off the gas, moving my foot to tap on the brake. I expect the bike to slow down so that I can take the corner at a reduced speed—just like the blue one did when Logan was driving—but instead it starts shaking. At first, I wonder if maybe I'm just hitting a series of potholes, but then the shaking turns violent, and I realize that this just doesn't feel right. I don't know what I'm doing wrong, so I hit the brakes hard and tighten my grip on the handle. But it doesn't matter . . . I'm at the corner now and moving too fast.

I turn the handle and lean hard to the left, trying to slow in time for the turn. The front of the bike jerks hard and goes down, like it's fallen into a big hole.

I fly over it to the right, and the bike goes with me, rolling.

Hundreds of pounds of steel and motor roll over top of me, the air in my lungs smashing right out. My shoulder screams in pain as the bike completes its course, landing next to me on its side. My left foot is twisted, stuck under the foot peg.

I gasp for air. My lungs burn, refusing to expand. I try to sit up, get my foot out from under the bike, but my right shoulder throbs with pain.

I lie there for what seems like hours, gasping, until footsteps sound near me. "Harper!"

I look up as Logan drops to his knees next to me. "Are you okay?"

I can't breathe well enough to speak, so I just nod. The grass is cold, tickling the skin on my neck that's not covered by the helmet.

Logan looks me up and down, realizes the bike is still resting on my foot, and stands up, trying to shove it.

Another engine roars, loud, and then Bick's there too, jumping off his quad, running to mine to help Logan roll it off my foot.

"What the hell happened?" Bick asks, crouching down. He goes to touch me, but stops himself, as if not sure he won't break me.

I manage a weak smile. "I don't know," I say, wheezing. "One minute I was riding and then the next it just went down."

"The wheel came off," Logan says, dropping down on my other side. "Can we help you up? Can you walk?"

I look over at the quad. It sits crookedly, leaning forward at a funny angle.

"What do you mean, the wheel came off?" I sit up, gasping at the pain that tears down my arm. "Owwwwww. I think I broke something," I say, through clenched teeth.

Logan loops his arm around my waist, pulls me to my feet.

"The wheel," he says, pointing. It's rolled all the way to the fence line, where it leans against the barbwire.

"I don't get it," I say, dizzy now, either from the pain or the loss of oxygen or both. I can't seem to grasp the theory of a wheel flying off on its own.

"I don't either," says Bick, shaking his head. The expression on his face has me worried that my condition is even worse than it seems.

"Come on, let's get you in," Logan says, scooping me up, cradling me in his arms like a baby.

"I'm not an invalid," I protest, as the world spins and tilts on end.

"No, you're hurt. I'm taking you to the hospital."

I lean my temple against Logan's chest and close my eyes as he carries me across the wide field, bigger than three football fields. Every step he takes jars my shoulder, and the pain comes off me in waves. Behind us, Bick's quad roars to life again, and then he's gliding along beside us, his helmet left behind somewhere.

Footsteps sound out, and I open my eyes to see Adam and Allie jogging over to us.

"Oh my God, are you okay?" Allie asks, her face flushed.

"I should call your dad," Adam says, flipping his phone open.

"He won't answer," I say.

"I know, but I'll leave him a message and then me and Allie can go to your house and tell him what happened."

"That's a good idea," says Logan, his voice deep and rumbly, with my ear resting on his shoulder like it is. "Tell him to meet us at the hospital."

"Sure." Adam nods, then turns away as he starts talking into the phone.

I'm right: it's an answering machine.

Bick jumps off his quad, then jogs across the driveway as Logan carries me across the gravel. Bick opens the door to the Jeep and holds it as Logan sets me gently down inside. "Do you need me to do anything?" Bick asks, standing anxiously to the side.

I open my mouth to speak, but Logan beats me to it. "No, just go take care of your bikes. We'll call you as soon as we know if anything's broken," Logan says, his voice authoritative, in control. It calms me, somehow. I relax into the seat as Logan buckles my seatbelt.

I close my eyes and rest my head against the seatback. "I'm okay," I mumble, hoping to reassure Bick. Behind him, Allie and Adam are climbing into Adam's car, off on their quest to find my dad.

Logan shuts my door, and moments later he's in his own seat, slamming his door and starting the car, and then we're pulling out of Bick's driveway, heading to the hospital.

CHAPTER TEN

I lean forward, wincing as Logan slides my favorite pillow behind my back, then pulls a comfortable old quilt over my legs. I'm not sure I noticed, until now, just how much this couch sinks when I lay down on it.

"That better?"

"Uh-huh." I settle back into the cushions, wiggling around so that the Velcro on my new brace doesn't rub on my shoulder blades. Thanks to a few X-rays, I now know that I have a broken collarbone. Six weeks of this ugly brace and I should be good as new. "Um, Logan?"

"Yeah?"

"Sorry about my dad freaking out on you."

Logan sighs, taking a seat at the other end of the couch and pulling my feet onto his lap. "You heard that?"

"You didn't close the door when you stepped out into the hall."

"Oh," Logan says. "It's okay, though. He didn't say anything

I wasn't thinking. I should have protected you, and I put you in harm's way. He was just worried."

"Scared," I correct. Even though I couldn't see my dad's face when he talked to Logan, I could hear his voice. And it sounded like he was barely holding it together.

"Of?" Logan asks, lightly rubbing the sole of my sock-clad foot. I'm suddenly glad I'm not wearing embarrassing mismatched or holey socks.

"Losing me," I say, staring at his fingers on my feet so that I don't have to meet his eyes. "Like he did my mom."

"I thought your mom died from a fall?"

I nod. "She did, but it could have been anything. See, my dad is like me. Not super adventurous, you know? My mom, she was different, always trying new things, never sitting still." I chew on my lip, fighting the rising pressure in my chest. "After my mom died, I could tell he was relieved that I became more like him. That he wouldn't have to worry about me the way he did about her."

"You can't live in fear," Logan says. "You could die from crossing the street or eating a bad cantaloupe."

"I know. That's why I appreciate what you're doing for me. My dad will come around."

The conversation falls away, and I close my eyes for a moment, concentrating on the small circles Logan is rubbing on the bottom of my feet. When I finally open them, I'm surprised to see the droplets of rain streaking down the windows.

"So much for our sunny day, huh?" I say, nodding toward

the window. Dark clouds have moved in since I left Bick's house three hours ago.

Logan slides out from under my feet and walks to the window, staring out for a long moment. "What is with this town? Every time I turn around, it's stormy."

"October's always like that. It's the Cascades. They trap the clouds here instead of letting them move over to Eastern Washington."

"Oh," he says. He finally turns back to me. "I should probably get going. Can I get you anything else? Water maybe?"

"Nah, I'm okay. I just took some pain pills so they'll kick in soon."

Logan walks to the coffee table and pushes it closer, then arranges the remotes so they're all within reach. Or they would be, if my arm wasn't in a sling. I don't point this out to him, because I find the gesture to be totally sweet.

"You think your dad will actually remember to check on you like he said? I don't want to leave you alone."

"He's just out in the barns. I know where he's at if I need him."

Logan nods and goes back to the window. A moment later, headlights splash across the wall. "Allie's here," he says.

"Really?"

I start to sit up, then wince again as my shoulder screams in protest.

"Yeah. She texted you a couple hours ago, while you were in X-ray. I told her you'd be released soon."

Moments later, the front door swings open. Allie appears,

holding a giant casserole dish. "So, my mom found out you went to the hospital and made you tuna casserole. It's probably disgusting."

I giggle, and it shakes my shoulder, sending a fresh wave of pain down my body. "Ow. Don't make me laugh."

Outside, the rain thickens, until I can hear the hum of it on the roof. Logan turns and stares out at the half-obscured glass. "I guess I better go. You guys sure you'll be okay?"

Allie reaches into her purse. "I brought *Titanic*. We're good for a few hours at least."

Logan smiles, then walks back over to me and kisses me on the forehead. "All right. I'll leave you girls to it." Then, turning back to me, he says, "Text me later?"

"Mm-hmm," I reply, watching as Allie crosses the room and slides open our DVD player.

"Okay then. Have a good one."

And like that he's gone, just as the rain really picks up. When the door swings open, the sound of it is positively roaring.

"Kinda sick of this weather," Allie says, dropping the DVD into the slot and pushing the mechanism closed.

"Yeah. It's getting old."

"Do you have popcorn?" she asks, turning the TV on.

"Yep, it's in the drawer to the right of the kitchen sink."

"Cool. Be right back," she says, strolling out of the room.

I try to remember the last time we had a chance to sit through the whole *Titanic* movie, but I can't. It must have been at least a year ago . . . before she got together with Adam.

I watch Logan's headlights in the window as he pulls out.

He's been amazing today, holding my hand at the hospital, waiting for hours while I got X-rays, listening to my dad rant about how he's supposed to watch out for me, not get me hurt. And he did it all without the blink of an eye.

By the time Allie returns with the popcorn, the movie is rolling. Allie plunks down on the worn-out leather loveseat, handing me my own small bowl.

It's a little awkward, holding the bowl with my sling-clad hand and eating with the other. Getting used to this is going to suck.

"I forgot how much I love this movie," Allie says. "Leo is so hot in it."

I lay my head against the pillow, tossing a few pieces of popcorn in my mouth. "I think he's cuter now. He's too baby-faced in this movie. Kate Winslet totally outshines him."

"No way. He's smokin'," Allie says, twisting around on the couch so her legs are up against the back and her head's upside down. Her own little popcorn bowl rests on her stomach.

I snort. "He's maybe a seven. She's definitely a ten. I'd give anything to look like her."

Allie twists around and sits up, setting her bowl down on the coffee table. "You're at least as hot as her, you just don't have all the smoke and mirrors. A makeup artist and a good stylist, you'd look better than she does."

I laugh. "Yeah, right."

"Seriously." Allie lights up. "Actually, my makeup is in the car. Let me give you a makeover."

I stop chewing and stare at her, realizing she's serious. "No way," I say.

"Come on! You totally owe me."

"For what?"

"For riding quads because *Logan* asked you, and not the thousand times I suggested it," she says. I can't tell if she's being playful or serious. Maybe Bick wasn't the only one bothered by my sudden change of heart.

I do kind of feel bad about riding quads for Logan and not for them—even if I ended up getting injured—but she just doesn't understand that things are different with him. He knows about my fears, and he's helping with them. Allie means well, and she's an amazing friend, but there are times I need her and she's too involved with Adam to notice.

I look back at the movie, watching as Kate Winslet climbs over the railing on the boat, her hair flowing out around her in the ocean breeze. "You can't really think I'd look that good."

Allie slides forward on the couch, steepling her hands. "Please please please please please? Just give me a chance. It's not like you have anything else on your oh-so-full agenda. You're practically an invalid."

I snort, and she grins sheepishly at me.

"Okay. Fine. Let's do it."

She squeals and claps her hands together. "I promise you won't regret it."

Except I might already.

CHAPTER ELEVEN

"Sit still!" Allie says, unwinding my smoking hair from the curling iron she just-so-happened to find in her car. If I didn't know better, I'd think she planned it. Maybe she thought I'd be so hopped up on medicine I would somehow not notice a stealth makeover.

I watch my nose scrunch up in the bathroom mirror. I'm afraid to look at the charred remains of my hair. "Are you sure it's supposed to smoke like that?"

"It's not smoke. It's steam. I put some product in it," she says, indignant.

"Steam. Right." I shift my weight on the old wooden stool and chew on the inside of my cheek, rethinking this whole idea. "What if I show up at school tomorrow with half of my hair missing? I'm *sure* Logan would be super attracted to me then."

She flinches, stares at my hair as if I said she just screwed it all up. "What?" I ask, my mouth going dry. I knew I would regret this.

"Nothing," she says, not meeting my eyes in the mirror.

"I really don't like that expression when you're burning my hair off."

"I told you, it's all normal. You really should do this stuff more often. Then you'd know."

"Hey, I managed to snag Logan," I say.

"Yeah, though God knows how," she says, grinning slyly. "It was a Sunday morning, which means two things: You probably fed the calves first and you totally smelled like a farm, and you were still wearing your pajamas."

I giggle. "Hey! I shouldn't be required to wear actual clothes until after I've had my Sunday morning donut. It's not my fault I ran into a cute boy at the bakery." I look up at her in the mirror, at her wide eyes framed by smoky makeup and thick mascara-clad lashes that curl perfectly upward. I want to ask her how she learned this stuff, if her mom bought her her first makeup and showed her how to put it on, but I don't. That would only lead to a discussion of my own mom. And I don't talk about her. Not with Allie and Adam and Bick, and definitely not with my dad.

"I was joking," she says.

"I know, but I question it enough as it is."

"You do not."

I shrug. "Sometimes. Don't you ever see us together and think, *Wow, he is so out of her league*?"

"No way. I've seen the way he looks at you. Anyone who sees that wouldn't question it."

I smile a little, staring down at my chipped nails. "Thanks.

I just psych myself out sometimes. He seems too good to be true."

"Except that whole secret twin thing," she says.

I twist my hands in my lap. "Yeah, sorry, I was going to talk to you about it, we've just both been so busy. Did Bick tell you about him?"

"Yeah. While you were riding quads. Just before you wrecked, that is. That's some crazy stuff." Allie unwinds another piece of hair, then sets the iron down and fluffs it up a little bit with her finger. I have to admit, it's really pretty.

I adjust my sling. It's already chafing my neck. The next six weeks are not going to be fun. "Yeah. I wasn't sure if I should be okay with it or not."

"Do you want a little bit of advice?" Allie asks, picking up the curling iron again.

I don't know. Do I? I've already decided to just forget about it. "Yeah. Um, sure."

She smiles, her pretty glossed lips turning upward as she winds another piece of hair up. "Forgive him. Guys screw up. A lot. You just have to figure out whether their heart is in the right place."

"And his was?" I pull away, my hair slipping off the iron.

"Hold still, will you? I'm almost done." She frowns, picks up the hair again, and twists it around the barrel. "Anyway, he was afraid of you rejecting him for the wrong reasons. He shouldn't have lied, but he did it because he didn't want to lose you. It seems like you've already kinda let it go. But if you haven't, you should."

I purse my lips and nod, surprisingly relieved. I wanted her to say this. Wanted her to say I was right for giving him another chance.

And she's right. Logan's been the perfect boyfriend, other than the whole Daemon thing. "Okay. Letting it go. Officially."

"You look amazing," Allie says, untwisting the final curl from the iron.

I stare at my almost unrecognizable reflection in the mirror. My flat brown hair has been transformed into pretty, glossy ringlets. I tug at one, and it bounces back into a tight curl.

"You really think so?"

Allie tips her head to the side and stares at me in the mirror. "Yeah. And I have an idea."

Allie and I sit side by side on the couch, me struggling to find a comfortable way to arrange my brace as she leans over and clicks on my bookmarks, bringing up my Facebook page. My profile picture is from last year. Allie and I are hugging, standing in front of a long stretch of pretty white fences, as a summer breeze lifts our hair out of our faces. Her mom snapped the picture of us at their house on a sunny day, the sky a vibrant blue. "This is so overdue," she says.

I nod, a little unsure. The pictures she took today—of me with curled hair, makeup done up—are pretty. I just don't know if they're too over the top to be the best profile pics. What if everyone thinks I'm trying too hard? I'd never wear this much makeup to school.

"Seriously. Live a little. Sex it up," she practically exclaims.

"You're always stuck in your little box."

"That's what Logan always says."

"What?" she asks, distracted. She's too busy clicking on buttons in a desperate attempt to transform my profile page.

"That I'm stuck in a box," I say. "He's trying to break me out of it, or whatever. That's why I was willing to ride quads."

"Well . . ." her voice trails off. "You *could* use a little excitement."

"Uh? What do you call dead birds in the school parking lot, a bloody handprint on the window of my car, a quad accident, and a boyfriend with a secret twin brother who got a kick out of freaking me out?" I ask, reaching up to adjust the Velcro on my sling.

"That's not the kind of excitement I'm talking about," she says. She gives me a skeptical look before glancing back at the screen and clicking to upload the photos.

It only takes a moment to upload a half-dozen photos Allie took in the last half hour. Looking at the shots onscreen, it's clear that she did a good job of it too, totally avoiding the ugly cotton brace. No one who sees the pictures will even know my collarbone is broken.

"This way, when Logan looks at his Facebook page, he remembers how hot his girlfriend is," she says, grinning.

Moments later, she's resetting my profile pic to one where I'm leaned back, my curly hair fanned out around me on the floor. I have a sorta-sweet, sorta-devilish smile on my face, and I'm looking up to the left. I'm not quite sure how she caught that look, but it's perfect. Flirty and mysterious.

She clicks over to my profile, as if to confirm it looks right, and then sits back abruptly.

"Whoa." She glances over at me, a nervous look in her eyes.

"What?" I sit forward, lean in to the small laptop screen.

Logan's user picture dominates my Facebook wall. Comment after comment. All just posted within the last few minutes.

Your profile picture makes you look frigid. And your friend looks way hotter than you.

You should invest in some blinds for your bedroom window, btw. I can watch you from the street.

I meet Allie's eyes and neither of us speaks. Why would he say that? Is he spying on me?

She pulls up the notifications and I see that he's been commenting on photos, too.

"Let's just delete them, okay?" She clicks on the first notification and it brings up a photo from last fall.

Someone put on a little bit of weight, he wrote.

A lump grows in my throat, and I cover my mouth.

Allie reaches over, rubs my back softly. "It can't be him, right? Someone hacked his page or something."

I can't stop staring at *my boyfriend's* photo next to such cruel, angry words. Allie deletes the comment and goes to the next one, deleting it before I can see what he wrote.

"It could be his brother," she says.

I nod, swallowing down the tears. "Yeah. You think?"

"Totally. There's no way Logan would say that stuff to you. Just no way. And he was just here. Look at the time stamps.

He would have had to literally race home, immediately log on, and start posting these. He wouldn't have done that."

I nod, pull my hands away from my face, nodding. "Yeah. You're right. It's gotta be Daemon or something."

"No 'or something.' It *must* be him. There's no other explanation."

"Right."

"Let's just see what else Daemon has been up to." She clicks on Logan's—hacked?—profile. The latest activity is simple:

Logan commented on Harper's wall.

Yeah, he sure did.

Allie scrolls down, then goes back up and clicks on his information tab, then scrolls around again. The whole thing is surprisingly sparse.

"You know, leaving the whole Daemon thing aside, it's kind of weird that Logan only has eighteen friends," she says, giving me a skeptical look.

I pull on one of the curls Allie did. It's already deflating, hanging down around my shoulders. I didn't have the right hairspray, I guess. "Well, he just moved here."

She chews on her lip and stares at the computer, then leans forward and scrolls for a while. "But his updates go back months."

"So?"

"So . . . he had this page when he lived in Cedar Cove."

Oh. The implications of her words finally sink in. I swallow the anxiety rising in my throat. "Who's on his friends list?"

She clicks on the list and scrolls through them. "Me, you, Adam, Bick . . ."

I sit forward, cradling my arm as we go over the list, both of us silent as familiar names scroll by. "They're all from Enumclaw," I finally say, when she gets to the end. "I don't get it. Does this mean he didn't have any friends in Cedar Cove?"

She purses her lips, glancing at the screen before turning back to me. There's something unreadable in her expression. "Either that . . . or he unfriended them."

My stomach hollows out. I hadn't even considered that.

She goes back to his wall, scanning his updates. Stuff about watching *Fringe*, something about a ball game, a picture update. All normal stuff. Probably not stuff that Daemon did. But nothing to tell us about Logan's life in Cedar Cove.

I wait with bated breath as she scrolls further down the page, deeper and deeper into Logan's past.

When she's back several months, there are several "Likes" on his status updates. She clicks on a few, the mouse hovering over names I don't recognize, people he's not friends with anymore.

She clicks back to his wall and scrolls further and further, until other things start popping up in his feed. Friend comments.

Ex-friend comments, since they're from names I don't recognize, people no longer on his friends list.

The first comes from a guy named Spencer saying, "Dude, last weekend was a blast!" followed by a girl saying, "Congrats! You killed it today."

Allie stops, glancing up at me. I just nod.

She right-clicks on the girl's name and uses the drop-down menu to open up her profile in a separate tab.

I sit back and watch as she scrolls further, opening up new tabs for a few other people from Logan's past.

"So he unfriended at least six people?" I ask, furrowing my brow. Why doesn't he want to be associated with people he was clearly friends with?

The first two girls and one guy all have private profiles, so they're no help beyond confirming their location—Cedar Cove, Oregon.

The next girl, a brunette with a smile that could melt the ice caps, has an open profile. She's from Cedar Cove, too. Allie scrolls down a bit to look for any comments from Logan, but we don't find any.

I lean in again as Allie scrolls back to the top of the page and clicks on the girl's photos.

There's an album marked "Fun stuff." Allie pops it open.

"She's cute," Allie says. Then she cringes. We both know this girl might be Logan's ex-girlfriend. "I mean, kind of."

I scan over her photos and see mostly female friends and what must be her dog. "Go back to the albums."

Allie clicks the back button.

"Go to that one," I say, pointing to the album labeled "mobile uploads."

And then, sure enough, there he is . . . Logan. My heart thumps when my gaze lands on his familiar face. Allie and I exchange a look, and she clicks on the thumbnail to enlarge the photo.

When she zooms in, I realize it's not just a group shot, but a *couples* shot. He has his arm around the brunette. She looks amazing in a slinky silver dress. Tall, lithe, ballerina-like.

My breathing turns shallow as I stare at the place where his fingers touch her bare shoulder, thinking of all the times he's held me.

I shake my head. This was months ago. *Months* ago. I don't need to get upset. I shouldn't get upset. I'm doing this to myself, after all. Digging into his past. I have to be prepared for what I might find. And an ex-girlfriend who he never talks about anymore isn't exactly *that* terrible . . .

"I don't get it," Allie says, staring down at the photo.

"What?"

"Well." She turns to me. "The whole point of Facebook is you can keep in contact with people you don't always see in real life. I mean, my mom friended half her sorority house from twenty years ago. There's no reason to delete all of your friends just because you move away."

I search for an answer. "Maybe they all know Daemon. He told me he wanted to distance himself from his brother. Daemon has a pretty bad reputation, you know?"

Allie stares down at the monitor for a moment longer before meeting my eyes. "What if he wanted to distance himself from his *own* reputation?"

I evade her look, instead reading the photo's caption. *Prom* is all it says. But there are people tagged. Logan isn't one of them. Why didn't they tag him? Or did he un-tag himself? If he did, that must mean that he doesn't want any of his new friends—including me—to see this photo.

"I don't know," I say, my voice soft. None of this makes sense.

"Hmm," Allie says under her breath. She turns back to the computer, her mouse hovering over the names in the tagged section.

Twenty minutes later, Allie snaps my laptop shut and sits back.

Neither of us speaks for a long stretch of time.

I don't know if it's the quasi-concussion I got from the accident or this whole Facebook thing, but my head is pounding harder than ever.

"Okay, so what do we know?" Allie says, finally breaking the silence.

I shrug my good shoulder, avoiding her eyes. I don't know how to feel right now. Upset? Embarrassed? I just learned more about my boyfriend's life in Cedar Cove by investigating on Facebook than I have in a month of dating.

"Harper . . ." Allie urges. "Let's figure this out."

I begrudgingly answer, "Okay, so he's had Facebook for at least a year. He moved here, and then unfriended all of his old friends, untagged himself from all their photos, and deleted their comments."

"We just don't know why he'd do that."

I nod.

"You know," Allie says, "it could just be really simple. Maybe Daemon did something to them, and maybe *they* unfriended *Logan* because they didn't want anything to do with his brother."

Relief whooshes through me. "That makes perfect sense. Logan said Daemon completely screwed things up for him in Cedar Cove. So whatever he did, it extended to Logan's friendships."

Allie nods. "Exactly. So what did Daemon do?"

I shake my head. "I don't know. Logan tried to tell me about him, but I was too ticked off he'd kept Daemon a secret, so I wasn't listening."

Allie chews on her bottom lip, staring at the closed laptop. "I think Logan needs to tell you about what happened in Oregon, and then maybe you two should have a sit-down with Daemon."

I pull the throw-blanket hanging on the couch over my lap, curling up underneath it. "Why?"

"Because obviously Daemon ruined Logan's relationships before. You two need to sit down with him and make it clear you're not going anywhere, and that it's not cool for him to mess with you like he obviously just did on Facebook and like he did the other day at their house."

I stare down at the orange blanket, picking at the little yarn pieces sticking up all over. "I don't know. You didn't see him fawning all over that gross stuff in the basement. I doubt a talk would just solve everything . . ."

"Harper!" Allie chastises me. "Don't just come up with excuses. This is a good first step."

I sigh. "Okay, you think that if we sit down with him in a

cool, collected way, we can reason with him, make sure he understands that Logan and I are together, and he needs to back off?"

"Exactly."

"Fine, but I seriously don't know if I want to see him again," I admit. "He scared the hell out of me before. There's something wrong with him."

Allie raises her brows, giving me a *duh* kind of look. "That's why it needs to be done."

"All right," I say, sinking into the sagging couch. I wish it would just swallow me up. I'm not relishing the idea of seeing Daemon again. But if he messed up Logan's relationship last time, he could do it again. He needs to know this time is different—that I actually want to stick around long enough to have something real with Logan. His harassing me needs to stop.

"I should probably go home," Allie says, standing. "Want me to put the casserole in the oven for you?"

"Sure," I say. "My dad will be in soon, and he'll be hungry."

She disappears into the kitchen for a moment and then pops up again. "God this weather sucks," she says. "Your pasture looks like a lake."

She walks to the door and is just touching the doorknob when a screeching sound—coming from the road outside—tears through the air. She glances back at me and then yanks the door open and steps onto the porch. I toss the blanket off with my good hand and rush after her, cradling my arm, just in time to see a big red pickup fishtail, its taillights shining bright in the night. It screams through the intersection, sliding right past a large white van.

The van veers hard left, spins around, and skids to a stop next to the ditch. One more foot, and it would have gone in.

"Whoa," Allie says, breathless. "That was really close. Look how far that van skidded."

I nod, taking a deep breath to calm myself. I'd been sure I was about to witness a major accident. "He must have blown the stop sign."

Allie walks across the porch, peering out through the sheets of rain before turning back to me. "He couldn't have."

"Why not?" I step up beside her, closer to the veil of rainwater.

"The stop sign is gone."

CHAPTER TWELVE

W hen the rose falls out of my locker on Monday, a chill sweeps down my spine. It's got the same black ribbon as the other day, and again something's attached to it. I stare down at where it landed on the ground, and consider throwing it in the trashcan without looking at it.

But I can't. I have to know.

With trembling hands, I slide the thick paper out from the ribbon and unfold it. It's a picture of me. The curly-haired, made-over picture we just posted to my profile yesterday.

But my eyes are blacked out.

I fling the paper onto the floor, wishing I'd just left it there to begin with, and put a hand against my locker to steady myself, my other useless arm sitting uncomfortably in its sling. Someone printed a picture of me and blacked out my eyes.

What kind of sick joke is this supposed to be? If Daemon is doing this, what's the point? Is he trying to scare me away from Logan? Why does he even care if we're together?

"Something wrong?" Adam asks, stopping in front of me.

I point at the paper on the floor. Adam looks at me for a long moment and then scoops it up, unfolding it. His face goes white. "Where did you get this?"

I swallow, point at my locker.

"It must be a Halloween prank," he says, sounding only half-convinced. "Right?"

"Maybe . . ."

"You don't sound so sure." He places one hand against the lockers.

"Well, it was attached to a rose. The third one I've gotten." I stop myself before saying more.

"And?"

"And the last one had a poem about how I was being watched."

He steps closer, alarm flaring to life in his eyes. "Why didn't you tell me?!"

"Because I knew you'd get all worked up," I say. "Sometimes you like to play big brother, and I didn't want to deal with it."

"I *should* get all worked up. With everything happening in town, this is a big deal."

"This is hardly related to bloody cow bones and Peeping Toms."

"And dead birds, and red handprints . . ." Adam gives me a pointed look. "And someone stole a few dozen stop signs over the weekend. There are two missing on my road alone."

I frown. "Yeah, same with mine. Me and Allie saw a couple

people almost wreck," I say, staring at my locker door. "They replaced the sign already, though. Besides, a few roses have nothing to do with that stuff. It's just a joke." I don't tell Adam about the *real* bloody handprint on my car window. Lately, I just keep thinking I might have imagined it. That the paint was just drier on my door, and that's why it looked like a darker shade of red and didn't have the same plastic scent.

He puts a hand on my good shoulder and turns me to face him. "I was debating telling you this, but . . . we figured out that Bick's quad *was* sabotaged."

"What? Like how?" The wheel's magically falling off was one more thing that I was trying to just push from my mind.

"Someone messed with the lugnuts and stripped out the studs. The wheel was *supposed* to fall off."

I stare at him, my head spinning. "But it couldn't have been about me. How would someone know I was going to ride that specific quad? Or honestly, even ride a quad at all?"

Adam shrugs. "I don't know. If it's not about you, then that means someone's after Bick."

"No, that's crazy. Why would anyone ever want to do anything bad to Bick?"

Adam cocks his head to the side. "So you think you're the more likely target?"

I shake my head. I don't even know what to think anymore.

"Either way, I just want you to take this stuff seriously, okay? Report the roses."

"I will," I say, turning to slam my locker so that Adam can't see the duplicitous expression on my face. "I'll go to the office during lunch."

Adam narrows his eyes. "And the reason you can't go now is?"

"We have to work on our campaign during politics. It's due soon and we don't get a lot of group time."

"But you swear you'll go later?" Adam stares, waiting.

I nod yes, and am pleased to see that Adam buys the lie. There's no way I'm going to report it. If it *is* Daemon, then it's Logan I need to talk to, not the principal.

He smiles in relief. "Okay. But text me if you need me for anything."

"Well, since you're offering, how about a Diet Coke?" I grin.

Adam just shakes his head, but he's still smiling. "Just let me know how it goes."

"Fine. Now go to PE already. Nothing's going to happen at school."

"All right, later," he says, heading down the hall.

I turn away from him, staring at the closed door to my locker. How did someone open it? How'd they get my combo?

I shake my head, clearing away the troubling thoughts as I walk away from my locker. If a little white lie gets Adam off my back, I figure it can't hurt.

Once through the door to class, I make my way to my chair, plunking my stuff down on my desk. Too late, I realize I have to be a little more gentle. A wave of pain cascades down my bad arm, and I take in a sharp breath.

"Hey," Logan says, reaching over to tug at the drawstring on my hoodie, flashing me one of his gorgeous smiles.

"Hi," I say, trying not to think of Daemon, of red handprints, of black ribbon.

His eyes sweep over my brace. "Feeling okay? Did you and Allie do anything fun last night?"

Conflicted emotions swarm my stomach. *Yeah. I Facebook stalked you. And I didn't like what I saw.*

I answer his question with one of my own. "Can I ask you something?" I look down at my sling, picking at a piece of lint sticking to the fabric.

"Sure. Shoot."

"What did Daemon do to get expelled from Cedar Cove?" I ask, looking up.

Logan opens his mouth to respond, but before he can reply, Mr. Patricks walks to the front board. "Okay, guys, I need to see highlights for your campaign plans by the end of the day today. You'll have class time all week to work on your actual campaigns, and then they launch in full on Monday, with your speeches. So get to work."

Logan turns his desk around and I scoot over, so that I'm staring at him—but he's looking down at his binder.

"It's kind of a long story, and I don't really want to get into it at school. Another time, okay?" He looks up and grins in a way that's meant to be reassuring, but I can't help but picture a different smile. A smile meant for the girl in the slinky silver dress, a girl he's never talked about. A prom he's never mentioned.

"Um, sure. Whatever," I say, trying not to give away my annoyance. I just want to know what happened. Why is that such a big deal? But I guess if he doesn't want to talk about it here, I'll have to ask him later.

I pull out a sheet of paper, writing *Campaign Launch Plans* across the top, and our names on the right-hand side. I can't stop myself from wondering if he ever worked on a project with the other girl, if she ever wrote his name on a paper like I'm doing now.

Then I write, in block letters, *advertising*, jotting down ideas like *posters*, *fliers*, and *buttons* underneath.

Logan clears his throat. "So, um are you going to be ready for the speech?" I lean back against my chair and shake my head. "No. Not even close. I can't believe Mr. Patricks is making us speak in front of another social studies class."

"It won't be *that* bad . . ."

I roll my eyes. "Why did I agree to this again?"

Logan leans forward, looking straight into my eyes. "Because you can do this. I know it scares you, but when it's all over, you're going to be happy you took a risk, that you made a name for yourself."

"Right. Sure. You're going to be rethinking those grandiose ideas of yours when Madison or Lucas totally trumps me."

"Not true. You—"

I cut him off. "Nope. We're going to lose the bonus points on the final when I go down in flames." I give him a fake smile, then grip the pencil harder in my hand and glance over at my competition. Lucas is the democratic candidate, a guy whom

I've shared various classes with over the years. He's nice. Total presidential type—diplomatic and levelheaded, but knows what he's talking about. Madison's the one I'm really worried about. There's no way she's going to play fair. She'll probably give dirty politicians a run for their money.

Logan slides his hand across his desk, laying it over mine. "Seriously. You're going to be awesome. I know you can do it."

"May I just remind you that the last time you convinced me to confront a fear I broke my collarbone?"

I almost feel bad for saying it, because Logan cringes. It wasn't exactly his fault anyway. The bike was sabotaged. I wonder if Adam told him. . . .

"Yeah, I'm really sorry about that. Are you doing okay?"

Sure. Other than being freaked out over anonymous roses and bloody handprints and mysteriously stripped lug nuts.

I want to say it. I want to talk about everything that's happened and how it all makes me feel.

But then again, I don't. I'd rather the roses just didn't exist. And part of me thinks that if I ignore them and that stupid bike, everything will go away.

I give him the simplest answer. "Mostly. My shoulder hurts whenever I jar it. Which apparently, I do about thirty times an hour."

"Yikes," he says, furrowing his brow in sympathy. "Sorry."

I shrug, unintentionally illustrating my point, and wince. "You know what? Let's talk campaign stuff to distract me."

"Okay, if you insist." Logan slides the paper I'm working

on onto his desk, jotting down a few notes. "So, we're still focusing on extending break time, increasing lunch options, and targeting the students least likely to vote, right?"

"Yeah. That's what we turned in last week. Might as well stick with it."

I swallow. "Um, so . . . were you on Facebook much yesterday?"

Logan raises a brow. "Change of subject much?" He grins. "Not really. I checked it yesterday morning before we went riding. Why?"

I stare down at my binder, unable to meet his eyes. "Because someone has been leaving me messages using your profile. I got three new ones early this morning."

"What?" Logan's chair squeaks on the tile as he snaps to attention.

I glance over at Mr. Patricks, who has his back to me as he works on his computer. We're not supposed to have cell phones in his class, but I fish mine out of my pocket and pop open my Facebook application before showing it to Logan. "Here. Look."

Logan takes my phone and his face goes pale as he looks over the messages.

"Weird, right?"

"Yeah . . ." He slides the phone back to me, a shocked expression still on his face.

"Were you still logged into your account the last time you closed your laptop?"

"Oh." He blinks. "I don't know. Probably."

"So then these messages must be from Daemon," I say, tucking my cell into my pocket.

He leans forward on his elbows. "Yeah. I guess. I'm sorry. I'll talk to him, and I'll change my password and everything."

"Honestly, I think we need to sit down with him."

Logan looks away, stares at the front board, and for a long moment, I wonder if he's going to answer. Finally, he says, "Why?"

I shift my weight, and my plastic chair creaks beneath me. "Maybe if we go about it diplomatically, just sit down in a calm manner, he'll understand this stuff isn't okay."

Logan shakes his head. "He knows it isn't okay. But you met him. He kind of gets off on getting under other people's skin."

I swallow, thinking of the hook in the basement sliding along the back of my neck. It's not what Logan's talking about, of course, but it doesn't stop the image from constantly appearing in my head. "I know, but I really think we should. Please? It would make me feel better to tell him straight to his face that he needs to leave me alone, to stop . . . messing with me."

I cut myself off just before I'm about to accuse Daemon of sabotaging the quad. He couldn't have known I was going to ride that bike, so it can't be him. It can't. And yet I still wonder . . . Logan's lips thin. "I can do it for you."

"I'm serious, Logan." I cross my arms, awkwardly thanks to the brace. "I want to tell him to back off. Together."

Logan sighs and leans back in his chair, meeting my eyes. "Okay. We can try."

"How about this weekend?"

"I don't know if this weekend would really work . . ." Logan mumbles. "It's kind of short notice."

I give him a pointed look.

"Okay, okay," he says, chewing on his lip as he glances down at his hands. He sighs, resigned, and meets my eyes again. "Does Sunday work for you?"

I nod. "Sounds good. What time?"

"Six?" Logan says, fully giving in now. "We can do dinner. I'll show you my affinity for boiling noodles."

I grin. "Sounds impressive."

"It's an acquired skill," he says, nodding sagely.

"Okay then. It's a date."

"Great." He grins and slides the paper back in front of me.

I peek down at the assignment and take a deep breath in relief. A few more days and this freaking campaign will be the only thing I have left to worry about.

At lunch, Allie and I grab some snacks from the vending machine, and I glimpse over my shoulder to be sure Adam isn't watching us. I don't want him to ambush me and insist on the office visit. If I tell the principal about my suspicions, they'll have to talk to Logan. I just don't want to make his life harder than it is already.

Arms full of junk food, we head to the gym to help with the Halloween Masquerade, a place I know I'll never find Adam. He's not exactly made of school spirit. Today we're supposed to be making papier-mâché spiders that will be hanging from the ceiling. We duck into one of the art rooms, and I nearly groan aloud when I see Madison standing at the back, doling out supplies like a drill sergeant.

"Oh, just shoot me," I mutter.

Allie rolls her eyes. "She's not *that* bad," she says, under her breath as we approach.

"What did you do, trip on those clown feet of yours?" Madison asks, her eyes sweeping over the shoulder brace and sling.

"It was a four-wheeler accident," I say, though I don't know why. I don't owe her an explanation.

"Huh. Well, whatever. I guess you can help with one hand, just don't screw it up."

She thrusts some cardboard pieces at me, and I grab them with my good arm while Allie gathers up the paste and the newspaper. We settle at one of the long, high tables at the back and spread the stuff out.

"Do we have a pattern?" I ask, scrunching my brows as I stare at the stuff in front of us.

"No. We have a half hour and our imagination," she says, laughing under her breath. I'm not surprised she's getting into this. "I kind of think we should just focus on the body, and then use some oversized pipe cleaners for the legs."

"All right," I say, skeptically. "Sure."

"Okay. If you can shred the newspaper, I'll try to figure out our base structure." Allie holds up a thin piece of cardboard, bending it into something vaguely resembling a circle. She frowns, staring at it with her head tipped to the side.

I grab the first stack of newspaper and use my bad arm to hold the paper down and my good hand to clumsily rip thin strips.

"Have you seen Bick today?" Allie asks, reaching for a piece of tape.

"Nope," I say, shredding another strip of newspaper. "Why?"

Allie looks up from her cardboard. "He wasn't in biology, and we had a big test—it's for twenty percent of our grade. What's weird is that we were talking about how he'd already finished studying for it just before you arrived at his house yesterday, so I can't figure out why he didn't show up."

"Hmm," I say, glancing up at her. "That *is* kind of bizarre. I can text him."

I set the newspaper down and fish my cell out of my pocket, quickly typing in *Where are you?* before dropping it back on the table.

"Do you think this is enough?" I ask, gesturing to the pile of newspaper. Already my shoulder is throbbing.

Allie shakes her head. "No, I've done papier-mâché before. That'll barely cover two spider legs. Do at least twice as much."

I nod and slide another chunk of newspaper under my arm.

Allie pulls out a long stretch of tape and wrestles with getting it over a gap in her cardboard contraption. "So . . . how are you feeling about the big Townsend family get-together? I assume Logan agreed to it . . ."

"Yeah . . . he did. Thankfully."

"Huh?" Allie glances up from her cardboard. "Are you saying that he wasn't exactly into the plan at first?"

I shove a pile of shredded paper to the side of the table. "No, not really. But I don't think that just changing his password will be enough to get Daemon off my back."

"That's what I've been telling you!" Allie rolls her eyes. "But why the sudden total-and-complete agreement? Before it felt like you were basically just gonna ask me to shut up."

I look down at the next newspaper. "I got a third rose this morning. It had my new Facebook picture attached."

"Oh?"

"With my eyes blacked out."

"*Oh.*"

"Yeah," I say, sighing. "Completely creepy."

"You don't think Daemon's like, stalking you, do you?"

I cringe. "I have no idea. I mean, I'm sure he's not *actually* a stalker. He probably just wants to screw with me. Freak me out."

"This is serious," Allie says. "Maybe after you and Logan talk to him, if he doesn't back off, you should report all this stuff to the cops and get a restraining order or something."

I rip another piece of paper, thinking about how Allie and Adam are starting to sound alike. "Yeah, I don't know. I think we'll probably just talk to his uncle next if he doesn't stop being such a creep. Involving the cops seems kind of extreme."

"I guess." Allie sets down a rounded, taped mass of cardboard and steps back to stare at it.

My phone buzzes against the table. I pick it up, assuming that it'll be Logan confirming the details for Sunday, but then nearly drop it when I read the message.

"What? What does it say?"

"It's from Bick."

"Yeah? And?"

I hold my phone out.

I'm at the hospital.

CHAPTER THIRTEEN

"Turn right at the stop sign," I say, from the passenger seat, my hands gripping the warm pizza box.

The news that Bick got into a car accident last night somehow spread all over school even though I didn't tell anyone besides Allie and Logan about the text. But he said he was totally fine and that they're releasing him tonight. If anything, he made it sound like the worst part was how crazy his parents were driving him, so I insisted on picking him up and bringing him home.

"Okay, we almost there?" Logan flips his blinker on and comes to a stop at the shiny new sign.

My stomach drops when I look at it. I'm anxious to get to the hospital, but Bick said he didn't want visitors until six o'clock because he had some tests to run, so I talked Logan into distracting me until then.

I force myself to stay positive. "Not yet. Still a little while to go on my magical mystery tour!"

"All right, captain," Logan replies, grinning at me. Then he turns and heads further down the hill, around a ninety-degree corner, and then across the bridge.

"That's the Green River," I say, pointing down at the water rushing beneath the bridge. Beside us is a big red barn that was converted into apartments and a pretty white silo painted *Argus Farms*. It belongs on a postcard, with its green fields and red-and-white painted buildings.

"As in the Green River Killer?"

I shrug. Did he have to ask that? With everything going on, I so didn't need to think of that. "Yeah. But like I said, I don't think they ever found any bodies in this part. It was further upriver and downriver they did."

"That's . . . pleasant."

I snort. Pleasant. Spooky. Whatever. "It's right again," I say, pointing at the sign. On my lap, the pizza box warms my legs through the thick denim of my jeans.

Logan nods. "So, you're bringing me to the romantic, non-body-dumping portion of the river?"

I laugh. "Like I told you before, nobody around here even thinks about the Green River Killer anymore. Water under the, uh, bridge." I pause, realizing what I just said. "So to speak."

"See!" Logan exclaims. "Now that's why I picked you for the class project. You really have a way with words."

"Don't I?" I chuckle.

"So . . ." Logan drums on the steering wheel. "Can I ask where we're going yet?"

"Fine . . ." I sigh. "I'm bringing you to a state park. Flaming Geyser. It's kinda cool, if you're not expecting a fiery ball of flames."

I point to the park gate, and Logan turns right, heading through the entrance and across another bridge.

"And what, exactly, *should* I be expecting? Other than delicious pizza"—he points to my lap—"and the sheer absence of dead bodies."

"Something more akin to a pilot light." I shake my head. "I still can't believe you haven't come down here yet! You live right above it."

"I didn't even know there was a park down here." Logan winds through the narrow paved road, trees sprinkling the grassy fields on either side. We pass a little ranger shack, and then cruise down the road at a slow and steady ten miles per hour. To our left, a group of people are flying elaborate remote-control airplanes. We leave them behind, eventually gliding into a parking space where the road dead-ends at a white gate with a stop sign.

We open the pizza box and each take a slice, grabbing napkins to use as pseudo-plates.

"I'm so sorry I forgot my candles and fine china. If you'd like me to use the dome light to set the mood, I'm more than willing." Logan winks.

I nearly choke on my first bite of pizza and barely manage to use a napkin to stifle my oh-so-attractive coughing.

"So what's number six?" he asks, shaking his head as he takes a bite of pizza.

I swallow my food and take a sip of soda to clear my throat. "Ironically? Jeeping."

"And you're sitting in a Jeep! I've cured you already!"

I roll my eyes as I set the soda can down in the cup-holder.

"But seriously," he says, "You're afraid of four-by-fouring?"

"Yeah. Adam has a Samurai, and Bick has his big souped-up pickup. They love going to this place up in the hills, and Allie goes with them all the time. But I'm too freaked out to go."

"Would you go with me?" he asks, setting his pizza down on the napkin.

"Do you even know how?"

He nods. "Yeah. We used to go in Tillamook Forest, just outside of Cedar Cove. Me and a few other guys got pretty good at it."

"I don't know," I say. Is he talking about the guys I saw on Facebook? His old friends? I blink, pushing all Facebook-related impressions of Logan's past from my mind. "I just keep picturing the whole thing flipping over and crushing me."

He puts his hand over mine. "Hey. You can trust me."

I take in a deep breath. "The quad thing didn't work out so well," I remind him.

"It would have, if the wheel hadn't broken. You know it was fun while it lasted. I had no way of knowing the wheel would break off like that."

"Yeah, I know . . ." My voice trails off. We still haven't talked about the fact that the bike was sabotaged, though by now, Adam must have told him. I saw the way he looked when I showed him Daemon's Facebook messages. What would he do if Daemon actually messed with that quad?

"Harper?" Logan says, picking up on my doubt. "Is there something you're not telling me?"

"I wouldn't say that . . ."

"Then what is it?"

"I have to ask . . ." I stare down at my slice of pizza. "Do you think Daemon had anything to do with it?"

"With what?"

"The wheel."

"Harper," he says, his voice firm. "Look at me."

I tear my gaze away from my half-eaten dinner and meet his eyes. "Daemon wouldn't do that. He likes to mess with people, sure, but he's not going to hurt you physically."

"Swear?"

Logan nods. "I promise."

"Good," I say, relief wooshing through me. "And yeah. I'll go. Four-by-fouring, that is."

He grins. "Really?"

"Yeah."

He leans forward and kisses me, stealing my breath away, making me forget what we'd just been talking about.

Ten minutes later, we've both scarfed two pieces of pizza, and we're ready to move onto the walking portion of our distraction date. I glance at my watch. Still an hour before I can go pick up Bick.

I slide out of the car, round the back, and accept Logan's hand when he reaches out for me. We walk, side by side, down a narrow cement path that later turns to dirt. Orange and yellow leaves crunch beneath our feet, until the sound of the river's rushing water drowns out the rustling.

We pass the salmon ponds, round a corner, and then I say, "Ta-da!" with a flourish of my arm.

Logan peers into a small crater, to where a little flame dances.

He chews his lip. "It's like two inches tall."

"Three. I told you it's all about managing expectations." I laugh, feeling good for the first time in hours. If I were home, I'd just be worrying about Bick, my speech, Daemon . . . and a million other things. Somehow, just being with Logan changes me in every way that matters.

Logan slips his hand into mine, as if sensing that I'm thinking about him. "So *that* is the infamous flaming geyser, huh? Still kind of hard to believe."

"Believe it!" I shrug, my voice ringing out. "Come on, I'll show you the bubbling geyser."

"Let me guess: It's more like the tiny bubbles little kids blow than giant ones as seen on TV?" he asks, his eyes lit up. He's having as much fun as me. In a way, I'm glad Bick wanted me to wait until six to come visit. Logan and I needed this. Time to ourselves without all the problems with Daemon and the stress of school and the mystery of dead birds and red handprints.

I snort. "Something like that."

"Can we see the river first?"

"Sure." I zip up my jacket and pull my hood over my head

as we follow the sounds of rushing water. Then I grab Logan's hand and pull him along.

Logan happily trails after me, then blinks when a rain drop lands on his nose. "Is it seriously raining? *Again?*" he asks, studying the sky.

"I'm telling you: If you'd hoped for sunny weather, don't hold your breath. It'll be May before we see anything like that." I take another few buoyant steps, then feel a tug on my hand and realize Logan's stopped. "You coming or what?" I ask.

"You don't think we should go home? I don't want to get stuck out in a rainstorm."

"Nah, it'll be fine. A little drizzle and then it'll clear right up. Come on."

"Okay," he says, shifting his gaze from the gray sky to follow me to the river. We climb up on a large boulder, and then stare down at the frothing white water.

"It's not really green," he jokes.

"Yeah, actually, I'm not sure where the name comes from. The river we crossed over to get to the haunted maze is the White River. And there's a little town called Greenwater to the east. I guess people around here aren't that creative."

Thunder rumbles in the east, but it's so quiet, the storm must be miles and miles away.

I turn to Logan, and he slips his arms around my waist. I relax into him, forgetting about the thunder. "Wonder what would happen if you fell in right now," he says, one side of his lips curled up.

"Har har," I say, sarcastically.

"Do you think we should find out?" His fingers tighten on my waist, and he pushes ever so slightly.

My heart slams into my throat and I jerk back so quickly, I nearly fall off the rock. It's only Logan's hands on my waist that save me, and I slam into his chest so hard the pain in my shoulder makes me cry out.

"Whoa, are you okay?" Logan asks, holding me up.

"Why'd you do that?" I hiss, breathless from the pain as I push him away, cradling my already injured arm.

"I was just joking around," Logan says in a low voice. "Trying to get you to face your fears. I didn't think you'd react like that."

I take in a deep breath and fight the urge to glare at him. "How did you know that water is one of my fears?"

"I didn't. Not really . . ." His voice trails off. He gets a strange look on his face, like he's lost in another world, but then he meets my eyes again.

"It's number five. I can't swim. My mom wanted to take me to lessons, but then she—" I stop abruptly, then meet his eyes. I don't have to finish the sentence for him to know what I mean.

"Ohhh," Logan says, his face falling. "God, I'm sorry. I had no idea."

I turn away and step onto the path again, looking up at the sky to rein in my erratic heartbeat.

"Look. The rain stopped," I say, gesturing up to the sky. The heavy gray has lightened considerably, the masses of rain clouds rolling away to reveal tiny patches of blue.

"Mm-hmm." He steps down from the rock and slips his arm around my waist. "I'm a good swimmer, you know." He leans down, kissing my cheek. "This summer, I'll teach you how to swim."

I allow myself to picture the long, hot summer days stretching out before me, Logan's eyes sparkling with the reflection of the sun on the river. We're in the water, and he's wrapping his arms around me, his skin hot against the cold river water. I want it so badly it hurts.

"So how about this bubbling geyser?" he asks.

I just stare at him.

"Hey. Seriously, I'm sorry if I freaked you out. I had a good hold of you. You weren't going in."

I nod, letting go of my annoyance. He turns me toward him, leaning down to kiss me softly on the lips, and my irritation floats away.

We walk down the trail, hand in hand, and I try to relax, to not picture how the water frothed and gurgled when he playfully pushed me toward it.

We wind down the pathways, crossing a few little wooden bridges that creak pleasantly underneath us, until we finally end on a platform, leaning over the railing and peering into the water below.

"Okay, so I know I was supposed to manage my expectations or whatever, but that's not what I pictured when you said bubbles," he says.

The bottom of the creek bed has a gray, ashy sort of color, and tiny air bubbles sprout almost constantly, rise to the surface, and pop. It's a never-ending, constant stream of bubbling, like a champagne glass lined with mud.

"I told you it wasn't going to be that impressive."

"So then why are you smiling like that?"

I shrug. I hadn't even meant to smile, but there it is. "I dunno. Because I like being with you even if you sometimes have a kind of sick sense of humor. Isn't that enough?"

He steps closer and touches my chin with his pointer finger so that I look up at him. "I *really* like being with you."

And then he closes the gap, and we're standing there beside the bubbling geyser as his lips graze mine. The faintest flutter of a touch steals my breath away. My eyes slip shut and the world seems to give way beneath my feet.

Logan leans into me, until my back is against the wooden railing, the geyser fizzing behind us. His elbows rest on the railing, and I reach up, interlacing my fingers at the back of his neck. I pull him against me, and for one beautiful moment, it feels like we're one. Then it seems like it's just a heartbeat later that he's pulling back, but it must be longer because by then I'm practically panting, trying in vain to catch my breath.

Logan makes the breathing thing even more difficult when a second later, he reaches up and traces my cheek with his thumb. "So maybe it's more impressive than I thought."

CHAPTER FOURTEEN

A couple hours later, I wait impatiently at the elevator, slapping the up button again and again, even though it's already lit. Hospitals always feel so . . . uncomfortable to me. I can't stand in them without thinking of my mother. Without feeling an echo of the panic I'd felt that day. And now, they also remind me of my broken collarbone, of flying over the handlebars of the quad.

I just want to find Bick and get out of here.

The doors glide open and I slip inside the lift, hitting the button for the second floor at least three times in the hopes that will make the doors close faster. Of course, when they eventually do, I find myself wondering how many germs are crawling around on the buttons, how many sick people touched them.

It seems like forever later when the doors slide open, and I follow the arrows until I'm standing in front of room 223.

I knock on the door frame and then step inside to see

Bick sitting at the edge of the bed, dressed in street clothes—Carhartt jeans and a black T-shirt, plus his Romeo shoes. When my eyes meet his, my mouth goes dry.

"*Oh*," I say, my voice falling.

He has cuts over his eyebrow, and one black eye, plus a swollen, split lip. "It looks worse than it is."

"I hope so, because you look terrible."

He laughs, and then winces. "Ouch. Don't make me laugh."

"Would you rather I made you cry?"

He chuckles and shakes his head. "Thanks for picking me up. My mom was driving me insane, running around and fluffing my pillows and handing me ice chips."

"Well, I thought we'd make a nice pair, what with your charming face and my lovely brace here," I say.

He chuckles again and shakes his head. "Can we just get out of here?"

I grab the backpack off the couch. "Sure. Are you all discharged or whatever?"

He nods. "Yeah, my mom signed all the stuff when she brought me my change of clothes."

"Cool."

I start to swing the backpack over my good shoulder, but Bick lifts it off me. "I can carry this, gimpy."

"Whatever, crash," I say, leading him out the door.

"Hey, the wreck wasn't my fault," he says.

"It wasn't?" I turn back to him as I push the down key on the elevator pad. We're almost out of here. Just a few more moments . . .

"No. Somebody plowed right into me. All I saw was a big black SUV. It pushed me right into the ditch and my truck rolled onto its side."

"Oh my God," I say. "Do you think they were drunk?"

"I don't know," he says. "They were going fast as hell though. I hardly saw them coming and by then it was too late to move."

"Why don't you know? Did you get knocked out?" I grab a hold of the railing inside the elevator, using my good hand to hold me up. Bick completely downplayed this on the phone. He *rolled* his truck. It was not some teeny little fender bender.

No wonder his mom was fussing over him.

"No. Well, maybe, but only for a minute. I remember what song was playing when they plowed into me, and it was still playing when I came to." Bick reaches up, tenderly touching the abrasions on his forehead. "The other driver didn't stick around."

We step into the elevator and I stare at him in the harsh light of the lift. "It was a hit and run?"

He nods. "Yeah. Exactly."

"How'd you get out of your truck?"

"I had to climb out the passenger side door. By then someone else was there, and they called 911."

The elevator dings and we step into the hall. "So is your truck totaled?"

"Probably. My mom had it towed to our house but she said it looks pretty bad. I might be able to turn it into a four-by-fouring rig. Take off the fenders and everything." He frowns, furrowing his brow.

My shoes click on the sterile tile floors as we walk past the hospital gift shop and out into the suddenly cloudless day. "Wow. That sucks. I know you love the thing."

He nods. "Yeah. I just keep telling myself it could have been worse."

"True." We cross the lot to my little car, and I hold the door open for Bick.

"Thanks, Mom," he says, rolling his eyes.

I laugh under my breath as I round the driver's side. Then I climb in, snapping my seatbelt on. "Well, you're right. It *could* be worse."

"How's that?" he asks, wincing as he reaches for the seatbelt.

I hold up my right arm. "I could drive a stick. And then we'd both be screwed."

When we arrive at Bick's house, I park next to his mangled truck and barely manage to contain my shock—it's so much more twisted and crunched than I could have ever imagined. I knew he rolled it . . . but . . . *wow.*

We climb out of my coupe and I can't help but stare at the crushed metal, the shattered windshield, the cracked headlights as we round the back of the truck on our way to the door of Bick's house. Bick shuffles along quickly, obviously eager to move past the hulking reminder of his accident. I move to follow him, then pause at the right front fender, my heart going still. "Um, Bick?"

"Yeah?" he looks up from the door to his house, disappointment swimming in his eyes as he once again catches sight of

147

his prized truck. He obviously didn't realize it was in such poor shape.

"How long did you say you were unconscious?"

"A minute. Maybe two, tops." He gives up on the door and comes back to meet me.

"Long enough for someone to do this?" I ask, pointing to the truck.

A blood-red handprint is emblazoned on the fender.

CHAPTER FIFTEEN

On Saturday, Adam pulls into my driveway in his jacked-up Samurai, all smiles as he whoops out the window.

I roll my eyes, thinking it's probably crazy to go four-by-fouring today, with my broken collarbone and with the image of Bick's truck so fresh in my mind. But I told Logan I would, so I can't back down now. Allie gets out of Adam's car and slides her seat forward, making room for me to climb into the tiny backseat. I'm glad I won't have to be crammed back here for long—once we get to Logan's, I'll be riding with him.

"Ow," I say, as I thunk down too hard and jar my elbow. I lean my head against the vinyl window, staring out at the fields as we leave my house.

"Smooth move," Adam says, slamming his door shut.

I roll my eyes, ignoring his barb. "It's too bad Bick can't come with us. It seems wrong to go without him."

"He'll catch us next time," Adam replies.

Then Allie adds, "I doubt his mom would let him go even if his truck was workable right now anyway."

I nod and stare out the window, thinking that Bick's mom might have the right idea. It took a good half hour for me and Bick to remove the red handprint from his truck window—it was just paint, fortunately. Still, though, the mark burns in my brain, making me believe that the "accident" wasn't one at all, that the same person who caused it is the one who sabotaged his quad, and that maybe that same person is also the one who's doing all of the other crazy stuff around town.

I'm so caught up in my own thoughts that before I know it, we're at the winding road to Logan's house. I sit up as we pass the familiar, overgrown hedges.

Adam turns through the rusty iron gates, and we glide down the cracked concrete driveway, pulling up in front of Logan's gothic house.

"That is seriously the coolest place I've ever seen," Allie says, awed as she stares up at the three-story behemoth.

"I think it's kind of creepy," I say. My vision of the house will forever be tied to Daemon's dark sneer, to the image of the little twin girls with a tragic fate. I can't view it as just a house anymore.

Then again, Daemon's been on my mind a lot lately. Luckily, tomorrow is Sunday. The day of our sit-down with him. I'm dreading it, but I want answers. I can't stop wondering if he's responsible for the red handprints . . . and other things as well. Things like Bick's accident.

We *have* to confront him.

Adam jumps out and pushes his seat forward, and I climb out, happy I'll be sitting in the front seat of Logan's Jeep and not the sardine can known as the backseat of a Samurai. I stand in the driveway and look up at the mansion, shielding my eyes from the glare of the autumn sun.

An upstairs window is ajar, gray curtains flapping through the opening. I see a tall figure flash by and then there's Logan, popping out the front door, impossibly fast. I glance back up at the window to see if someone else is up there, but there's nothing but shadows.

"Hey," he says, leaning in to kiss me.

"Hey," I say. "Is that your uncle upstairs?"

Logan turns and looks up at the curtain as it flutters in the breeze. "No, he's away on business for a while. That's Daemon's room."

"Oh," I say. So Daemon showed me his own room, not Logan's, on the tour?

"So, you ready for this?"

I take in a ragged breath of air. "Sure. Number six. Four-by-fouring. I can totally do this."

He grins. "You're riding with me, right?"

I nod and follow him to his shiny red Jeep, glancing back to wave at Adam, who is supposed to lead us up some old back-roads to Evans Creek ORV Park, since Logan and I have never been up there. He climbs into his Samuari, taps his horn once, and turns his car around as I climb into Logan's Jeep.

We leave the creepy mansion behind and follow Adam down some back roads, across a bridge or two, up a winding, narrow road on the side of a mountain. Overgrown branches scrape at the vinyl windows as we snake between trees, around curves.

We stop at a tall, narrow bridge, waiting for a 1950s Chevy truck with rusty fenders to pass by. The bridge is hundreds of feet tall and only wide enough for one vehicle. Once we have the bridge to ourselves, we cross, sailing impossibly high over the Carbon River.

Somewhere along the way, while I'm staring up at the canopy of Evergreen trees, Logan's fingers find mine. I've craved his touch all week long, and finally, here we are.

"You never told me why Daemon got expelled from Cedar Cove," I say.

His warm touch turns awkward when he stares back out the windshield. When he slows for a curve, he has to untangle his fingers from mine and shift. "It's a long story," he says.

"It's a long drive," I say.

He purses his lips. "I know you want to know, but . . . I've spent the last year feeling like everyone looks at me differently just because of him—Daemon. And I can't take it anymore. I just don't want to talk about it right now," he says.

I look down, twisting my hands in my lap. "When will you?"

"I promise I'll tell you eventually. But can you please just trust me?"

"I already do, Logan. It's Daemon I don't trust. I want to know what he did."

"Can we talk about it after we're done Jeeping? We'll go get dinner or something."

"I guess. Yeah. Sure." I sigh, barely holding onto my patience.

"Good," he says, brightening. "Now, tell me: What's number four?"

I turn to him, and despite my earlier annoyance, find my lips curling into a smile. "Driving on the freeway."

"Seriously? You've never driven on the freeway?"

I shake my head. "I made my dad take me to Puyallup for my driver's test because I heard they only make you go on local roads."

"And?"

"And the rumors were true," I say, staring down the steep, jagged angles of the mountain. Maybe driving up a crazy, rutted backroad should have been on my list too. I feel like we could slide right down the hill, and we're not even to the off-road park yet.

"You've really never driven on the freeway? Ever?"

"Not once."

"Wow. I have to admire your persistence, at least," he says, grinning at me in a way that makes me forget that we're hundreds of feet up in the air, twisting and turning on a perilous mountain.

And that we're about to careen down it . . . intentionally.

We pull into the gravel lot by Evan's Creek, and Adam stops, gets out of his SUV, and then jogs back to Logan's window. Logan rolls it down, and Adam rests his forearms on the sill as he leans down. "We can go easy or challenging."

"Easy," I say, just as Logan says, "Challenging."

I turn and glare at him—only sort of kidding—and then look at Adam. "Come on, guys, I have a broken collarbone. Can't we just take some nice, leisurely trails?"

Logan and Adam share a look and I can't tell what it means, but before I can protest, Adam nods and heads back to his Samurai.

I swallow. "So you're doing easy, right?"

"You'll be fine, Harper. I promise. I won't let anything happen, okay?"

I take in another ragged breath of air and nod, willing myself to believe that even though this all feels really similar to the quad-riding episode, at least this time Logan will be with me til the very end. "Okay. Yeah. Let's just get this over with." I tighten my own seatbelt. Allie goes off-roading with Adam all the time and says it's a blast. If she can handle it, I can too.

Logan shifts into gear as Adam pulls out, heads between two fir trees, and disappears into the shadows.

We follow, splashing through a few puddles, the mud-brown water spraying out around us. Adam's black Samurai pulls away as Logan slows. The monstrous climb looms in front of us.

"We have to give him a little space on hill climbs," Logan explains. "If he gets in a tough spot, we don't want to be too close."

I nod, but I'm not sure whether I should feel relieved by the confidence in his voice or freaked out by the idea of being "in a tough spot." What does that even mean?

I can just see the flash of brake lights from Adam's black Samurai at the midway point in the climb, partially obscured by the new orange and yellow foliage on the deciduous trees.

"Logan?" I ask, my voice rising.

"I got it," he says.

"Oh." I try to imagine myself at home, relaxing on the couch, watching *Titanic* with Allie.

"Okay. We should be good," he says a long moment later. I ditch the vision of a comfy couch and grip the handle on the dashboard as Logan shifts into first gear, spinning his tires in the mud as we set off.

We hit the bottom of the hill at what feels like high speed, and I think I might fly right out of my seat. Halfway up, though, I realize he had to do that and that we're slowing as we climb higher, losing momentum.

I grip the door handle with white knuckles.

We hit a giant hole bordered by two large boulders and I nearly hit the ceiling, my hair flying up around me. I grimace, cradling my arm to protect my collarbone, but a moment later I change my mind and grab the handle again.

Logan hardly moves, and my fear ebbs. He's got one foot on the clutch and the other on the gas. Meanwhile, one of his hands is on the wheel and the other on the stick as he tries to make it out of the huge hole without hitting the boulder on my side. His face is serious, concentration taking over.

So he's really not a rookie. I unwind a little and relax my death grip on the handle.

Logan stares forward, tense as he grinds the gear—nearly

missing it all together—and then hits it and we lurch forward.

We get out of the hole and creep forward, and I slide back in my seat as we hit the steepest part of the climb. I hold my breath as Logan eases up the last stretch, ultimately lurching over the edge of the hill, where Adam's Samurai comes into view.

"Nice job," I say, punching Logan playfully in the shoulder.

"You say that as if you doubted me," he says, grinning.

I grin, feeling as if I'm literally on top of the world. "Nah. I knew you could do it."

He beams. "See? Another fear off the list. That wasn't so bad, right?"

"Yeah, yeah. It was actually kind of cool," I say. Adrenaline pumps through me, and I feel like I'm on a sugar high. That was incredible. Scary and boundary-pushing but incredible.

"Let's jump out and stretch our legs," Logan suggests, obviously aware that I'm going to need a moment to take it all in.

We climb out and stroll past Adam and Allie, who are still sitting in his Samurai, to a point where the trail curves.

I stop at the edge of the trail, and Logan steps up beside me, so close we're touching shoulders. Sunset is just beginning, the sky tinged with shades of violet and pink, highlighting the snow-capped peak just across the valley.

True, I can see Mt. Rainier from my own front yard—Enumclaw is the closest real town to Mt. Rainier National Park—but it's nothing like this. Here, it feels like I could touch it, toss a rock and have it land in the snow on the peak.

It's enormous, craggy, and rocky, beautiful, the snow reflecting the growing pink sunset.

"Wow," I say, breathless. "If I had known it was this pretty, I might have let you talk me into this sooner."

"Are you ready for round two or what?" Adam hollers from twenty feet away. "My spidey sense tells me that it might rain."

"What are you talking about?" I spin around and glare at Adam for breaking our romantic moment, but then I just roll my eyes when I realize he's literally hanging out the door of his Samurai. "All right, let's just get this done."

We go back to Logan's Jeep, and Logan seems to be shifting around a bit, uncomfortably. I look out the window and realize that sure enough, Adam was right—there *are* storm clouds building in the distance, just over the mountain peaks.

"Strange that we didn't notice those before," Logan says, echoing my thoughts.

"Don't worry," I say, hoping my voice comes across with more confidence than I feel. "They might get some lightning back in Enumclaw, but the darkest clouds are so far away, I'm sure the most we'll get here is a light drizzle."

Logan nods, but I'm not sure if he really buys my theory. We ride quietly down the flat side of the trail loop, which isn't nearly as hairy as the hill climb, and the pretty mountain peak disappears behind us.

Just up ahead, Adam taps his brakes, and then turns left, his Samurai disappearing between the trees. Logan turns in the same spot, then hits the brakes.

Below us, Adam's Samurai lurches down the hill, his brake

lights brightening here and there as he goes around giant holes and craggy rocks. Logan flicks on his wipers as raindrops dot the windshield, just as Adam predicted.

They squeak and whine across the glass as the Samurai disappears from view.

"Wow. That looks . . ." My voice trails off, and I wait for Logan to comfort me, talk me out of being freaked out, but he doesn't say anything.

Instead, he reaches for the stick.

"Don't you think you should give Adam more—"

But Logan's tires are already rolling over the ledge.

"Stop!" I say, stamping my foot down as if I have a brake on my side. I don't know anything about this stupid sport but this doesn't seem right. If Logan had to give Adam space going up a hill, wouldn't he need to going down too, especially now that it's raining?

I think I hear thunder, but I can't tell because the engine is too loud.

Logan doesn't speak, just shifts into *second*. Second gear? Down a hill this steep? Instinct tells me second gear is too fast. Fear streaks up my limbs, intertwines with my heart in a way that makes it hard to speak. "Slow down," I grind out through gritted teeth.

The Jeep glides faster and my heart climbs up my throat, as if it wants out of my body.

"Slow down!"

Logan doesn't acknowledge me. His dark eyes are unreadable, staring straight ahead. He's not even blinking.

He can't go down a hill like this in *second gear*. Is he freakin' suicidal? We're picking up speed, hitting rocks with such a hard jarring motion it sends waves of pain up my spine, and the ache in my shoulder spreads. The key ring jingles hard with each bump and I hang on so tightly my fingers ache.

"Logan!" I scream it at him, letting go of the handle to shove him hard, in an act of desperation, and he blinks, looks up at me with a look of utter confusion and shock.

He turns abruptly to look out the windshield and then he downshifts, hits the brakes. But it's too late. We're going too fast to regain control. The mountain's too steep here, the rocks and holes too big. The Jeep's tires lock up and we skid, Adam's Samurai looming close.

Logan tries to maneuver around a big rock, but it's impossible because he's going this fast. The right wheel and bumper catch on the edge of the rock and the momentum twists the Jeep until we're skidding down the trail sideways.

I scream and grab a hold of the handle, closing my eyes in paralyzing fear of what's to come next. I just know that when we hit another big hole, we're going to tip over, and we're going to roll.

The engine revs, tires spin.

Then we slam into something and the Jeep stops. The engine sputters, then dies, and there's nothing but silence. Waves of pain travel down my shoulder, like an echo of the hard hit we just took.

I'm afraid to open my eyes—if I do, I might see that I'm upside down somewhere or perched precariously at the edge of something. So I just breathe deeply and squeeze my eyes more tightly shut.

"What the hell!" Adam's voice rings out. I open my eyes just as my door opens and Adam's leaning in, his face etched with concern. "Are you okay?" he asks, his voice lower.

There's no part of me that's not shaking. We just came within a breath of rolling down the hill, tumbling end over end. I blink, take an unsteady breath. I want to tell Adam I'm okay, but it's all I can do just to breathe.

"What the fuck was that?" Adam asks, turning to Logan.

"I don't know, I just lost control—"

"Because you flew down the fucking mountain!" Adam screams, and then snaps his mouth shut for a moment, his chest heaving. He lowers his voice. "If you were trying to prove something, you shouldn't have let her ride with you." He turns to me. "Get out of the car, Harper. You're riding back with me."

I want to listen but I'm still trying to get my heartbeat under control.

"I don't think you have to—" Logan starts.

"If I hadn't stopped right there and *let you* ram into me, you would have hit that hole sideways and flipped. She's riding with me and that's final." Adam leans over me, unbuckles my belt, and all but lifts me from Logan's seat. I just stare back at Logan as I let go of the door and it swings shut on its own weight.

I nearly fall to the muddy ground once outside, but Adam grips my waist tighter. Now that I'm standing outside the door, I see how sideways the Jeep really is. It's banked at such a drastic angle that if Logan tries to open his door, it probably won't open more than halfway before hitting the dirt.

I start to digest what just happened—or at least the tail end of it—Adam intentionally stopped his rig to let us land against him. To keep us from flipping into the hole and tumbling down the mountain end over end.

By the time I get to Adam's Samurai, Allie's climbed into the back to make room for me. I slide into the front seat and buckle my belt with shaky hands. I stare straight out the dirty windshield, down the rest of the mountain, trying to imagine what it would have been like to roll down it like that. The Jeep has a roll cage but I don't know if it would have been enough.

"Stay put for a second," Adam says, outside. He's talking to Logan. "I'm going to get the girls to the bottom, then I'll come back and guide you out. Don't move until I get back."

"Got it," Logan says, his voice resigned. I wonder if he's looking at me through the rear window of the Samurai but I don't turn around.

Adam slides back into his seat, but doesn't immediately start the engine.

"You really okay?" Allie says, her voice low. "That was really scary."

I swallow and just nod, not quite ready to speak. Adam turns back to the steering wheel and I stare in a daze, immobile as he navigates the rest of the hill. We were only halfway down. The stumps and rocks and holes could have killed us if we'd rolled sideways like that. The Jeep would have been totaled.

At the bottom, Adam pulls to the side and parks under a maple tree. He climbs out of the Samurai, goes to the bottom of the trail, and starts climbing up on foot. A russet-colored leaf drifts silently down, lands on the hood of the car.

I sit in silence for a long moment, staring at the leaf, waiting for my heartbeat to go back to normal. It's only then that I realize the rain stopped, that the windshield is basically dry. "What happened?" Allie asks, quietly. She touches my shoulder.

I swallow, but don't look at her. The fear is only just ebbing. "I don't know. We were at the top and I thought he was going to wait—" My voice cracks. "But he just gunned it. I was screaming at him and he just kept going."

"Adam was freaking out. He saw you guys in the rearview and knew right away it was all wrong."

I nod. Up the hill, I can just barely hear Adam shouting orders at Logan, hear his engine revving, gears grinding. Long moments pass, and the sounds quiet and a set of headlights reflect in the side mirrors. He made it to the bottom.

Adam climbs into the Samurai without a word and we head down the gravel, Logan's headlights following.

No one suggests I get back into the car with him.

CHAPTER SIXTEEN

"I don't know what to say to him," I say, leaning against my white wooden headboard.

"Do you *want* to talk to him about it?" Allie asks, glancing up at me from where she sits on my bed, leaned over my toes, a nail polish brush in hand.

"Well yeah," I say, trying not to move and mess up her polish job. "He's my boyfriend. I just don't know what the hell was wrong with him. I've never even gone four-by-fouring and I knew what he was doing was wrong. If Adam hadn't been there . . ."

"Yeah, it was scary to watch." Allie reaches over to dip the brush into the bottle of nail polish on my windowsill. "This is a nice color on you," she says under her breath, slathering a pristine layer of baby blue polish on my right big toe.

"Thanks. What would you say to him if you were me? I've been avoiding his calls for the last twenty-four hours, but we have school tomorrow."

Allie moves to grab the bottle from its spot on the window ledge, then pauses as she catches sight of something outside. "I don't know, but you'd better figure it out quick, because he just pulled in."

I shift my weight, leaning forward on my elbows to look out the window, where Logan's Jeep has just come to a stop. The brake lights flicker and then turn off.

"I'm done with your nails anyway. Do you want me to stay or go?" Allie asks, capping the nail polish.

"Um, I guess you can go. I'll text you later," I say, standing and waddling to the door so I won't ruin the fresh polish on my right foot. "Thanks for coming over. I didn't really feel like being alone."

She twists the top on the nail polish, setting it down on my nightstand. "Yeah, of course."

We go down the steps and reach the back door just as Logan's about to knock.

Allie turns to me. "Okay, well, see you tomorrow in school then?"

When she leans in to hug me, she whispers, "Good luck" under her breath before pulling away. She opens the door and slips behind Logan without a word to him.

He doesn't move, just stands there, looking like a lost puppy. He clears his throat. "Can I come in?"

I nod and shrug, like I can't decide between the two.

He steps in, and I see something in his hands—leather-bound and thick. A chill sweeps down my spine as I think of the album Daemon showed me, but then I shake it away. This one is blue, clearly newer.

He stands three feet away, just inside the door, under the fluorescent lights of the kitchen. It's an awkward distance given the closeness between us. "I'm so sorry about what happened at Evans Creek. It would kill me if something had happened to you. If I had somehow hurt you."

I just stand there, one hand gripping the Formica countertop. I don't know what to say.

"I've been beating myself up all day about it."

I shrug.

"It's not okay, Harper. You could have been hurt."

I throw my hands up in the air. "Then why didn't you listen to me? I told you you were going too fast. I told you to slow down."

Logan nods. "I know. Once I stared down the hill, it was like . . . I was somewhere else." He swallows.

"What are you talking about, Logan? Where else could you have possibly been?"

He stares down at the linoleum floor, his eyes shuttered from view. "It was like I was in my mom's car. Plunging down the mountain."

It's like a rug being yanked out from under me. A wave of sorrow and surprise swoops through me, hollows out my stomach. I knew his mother died in a car accident, I just didn't put it together in my head. Maybe that's why Logan *gets* all my weird fears. Because his mom's death has given him at least one fear of his own, even if he doesn't admit it to himself. "*Oh.*"

He closes the distance between us, setting the photo album

down on the counter and touching my chin softly with one finger so that I have to look up to see into his eyes. "I don't know what I was doing. It was like my body went into auto-pilot and my head was back there, at the accident. I wasn't thinking. At all."

Abruptly, he pulls away, goes to the window. He leans his forehead against it and goes silent. "Look, I know you're the one with the list of fears, but I have them too. There's only one that haunts me."

I wait in silence.

"It's being alone. I lost my parents, and Daemon . . . well, he may as well be dead to me. You're all I have."

I look down at the photo album, noticing that a picture has been inserted into the cover. "Is that your mom?"

Logan turns away from the window, walks to the counter. "Yeah. At our first middle school soccer game."

"You played soccer?" I ask. Now his stick shift makes more sense. He actually is—or was—into sports. It feels weird that I didn't know that already. I feel like we've been together so long, but I met him less than two months ago.

He doesn't speak, simply slides the album closer to me, and we move to sit at the island counter, on side-by-side wooden stools. I look down at the cover, and a woman in her thir-ties stares back at me, smiling with a flawless smile just like Logan's. He and his brother stand on either side of their mom, in Kelly-green-and-white uniforms, each of them holding a soccer ball. Where Logan's hair is long, floppy as ever, his brother's hair looks shorter, more like a buzz cut.

"You had braces," I say, studying his metal-filled grin.

"Yeah. We both did," Logan replies. His voice is filled with nostalgic longing.

"He looks so much like you," I say, and then feel stupid. Of course he does. They're identical twins.

"Yeah. Still does." Logan raises his eyebrows.

"*Right*..." Daemon does look like Logan. So much so that I didn't even realize he wasn't my boyfriend when we met.

"Look," Logan continues. "I know I'm not an easy person to be with right now." His eyes are earnest. They beg my forgiveness. "I've gone through a lot. Daemon used to be different, you know? He had his issues, but he was never this messed up."

He looks down at the photo. "I lost them both, I just didn't know it until much later. I don't know if it was losing my mom, or his head injury, but he's not the same. And it's taken me a long time to realize it, but I have to live my own life. Separate myself from him and move on."

"Why is he so weird?" I ask, flipping the album open. It's Logan and Daemon as five- or six-year-olds, riding bikes side by side, smiles from ear to ear.

"My dad was tough on both of us, but he favored me. It didn't take a rocket scientist to figure it out. Daemon did everything he could to impress my dad, and it was never enough."

I flip to a page and see Logan holding a trophy.

"That was the last year we both did soccer. They split me and Daemon up onto different teams, and in the final game, we ended up playing against each other." Logan looks up and our eyes meet. "My dad cheered for me, Harper. Only me."

He looks back down and flips the page, and it's a birthday party, an enormous cake sitting between Daemon and Logan. "Our sixteenth birthday was three weeks later. My dad got us the same gifts, but afterward, he gave me a watch his father had given him. He said he only had one, and that it would have to be our secret."

"But it wasn't . . ."

He shakes his head. "Daemon found it a month later in my room. That was the final straw for him. He got into a screaming match with my dad, and they almost lost it. I thought they'd throw punches for sure."

"They didn't make up after that?"

Logan snaps the book shut. "My dad died two months later."

Oh. I rub my hand on Logan's arm. "How?"

"A heart attack," he says. "He was only forty-two."

Wow. I had no idea.

"All this just happened a year ago?" I ask.

"Yeah." He stares down at the photo album, chewing his lip.

"And your mom . . ."

"She just died eight months ago."

I can hear the loneliness, the heartbreak, in his voice. The pain is so recent, so close to the surface, big and gaping and raw.

"She was having such a hard time with my dad's death, and Daemon was getting into more and more trouble at school. My mom told us to pack an overnight bag and that we were going to stay at some nice place on the beach, just get away from it all for a little while."

"But you didn't make it," I say.

"No. It was storming, and the road we took was winding, with this rocky cliff side. A deer came out of nowhere and she swerved, and we went right off the edge. The car rolled twice and then hit a tree on the driver's side. It completely smashed where my mom was sitting. I came to a day later, in the hospital. She was gone, and I went from having a real family to . . ." His voice breaks. "To just me and Daemon."

"If this was last spring, why didn't you come to Enumclaw sooner?"

"We stayed with some friends in Cedar Cove until my uncle bought the house here. We finished out the last two months of our sophomore year in Oregon. Of course, Daemon still screwed that up and got expelled, which is why he's homeschooled now."

"I had no idea all this was so recent."

Logan twists his hands in his lap. "I know. I don't like to talk about it. But I couldn't let you think that I screwed up so badly at Evan's Creek because I'm reckless and don't care about you. All I want to do is to protect you." He turns toward me so our knees touch, pulling my hand into his lap. My head spins with the things he's saying, with the familiar feel of the warmth of his skin. "It was like I just . . . got lost in the memory of it. If you hadn't smacked my arm, snapped me out of it, I don't know what would have happened."

"Look at me," I say. When he looks up at me, I see the raw

pain swimming in his eyes. "I'm not going to go anywhere. But you need to be more honest with me about this stuff. I need to know you. Inside and out."

Logan nods.

"Why was he expelled?" I ask.

Logan is silent for a long moment, and I think he's going to refuse the question, but then he says, "There was a fight. At a party. It escalated, and some people got hurt. I'll tell you all the details, eventually. But can that just be enough for now?"

I purse my lips. I want to say no, want to push for more, but for the first time, Logan's giving me information, and I know I should let it all come out on its own time. He's already bared his soul enough for one day.

"Okay. But I still think we need to sit down with Daemon, demand that he stop harassing me. I got three more Facebook messages today. They need to stop."

"If you knew him, you wouldn't want to sit down with him at all."

"I met him that once. I know enough. But he needs to hear it from me—from both of us—that he has to leave us alone, that I'm not going anywhere." The solemn expression in Logan's eyes changes to one of relief. "And if he doesn't want to listen, we have to talk to your uncle or take another step."

"Really?" he asks.

"Really what?"

He leans in, his eyes so intense, so eager, I can't look away. "You're really not going anywhere?"

I smile back at him. "Of course not."

Logan twists on his stool, so our knees are touching. When his fingers find the back of my neck, gently pull me closer, I don't resist.

I lean in and kiss him, relishing the warmth of his lips. A long moment later, he rests his forehead against mine, staring into my eyes.

"You think you're alone, but my mom's gone too," I say, forcing my voice to remain level. "And my dad barely pays attention to me."

The silence stretches on for an excruciating moment, and Logan squeezes my knee. It's such a tiny gesture, and yet somehow, it means everything.

"So she was adventurous?" he asks, softly.

I nod. "Yeah. The polar opposite of me. I always took after my dad, and we basically watched her from the sidelines, you know?

He leans into me, pulls me against him, and I exhale a shaky breath.

"I need you as much as you need me," I say.

"Thank you," he says.

"For?"

"For seeing the real me and none of the bullshit. For opening yourself up to me. For being you."

I blush, feeling warm all over as I sink into him. We sit in silence for a while, the house dark and quiet, until my eyes are dry and we're just . . . comfortable again, no weird tension between us. He stands, pushing his stool back and standing.

"Can we take a raincheck on the Daemon meeting? I think you've had enough excitement. We can get together with him next weekend."

I purse my lips, nodding.

"Okay, well, I gotta get home, but I'll see you tomorrow at school, right?"

I sigh. "Yeah."

"Big day."

"Big speech," I say.

"You're going to be amazing." He kisses me one last time, then goes to the door. "Just remember. Picture everyone in their underwear."

I laugh, and it breaks the lingering tension.

"Okay then, later," he says, slipping out the front door.

I stand and walk to the window, watching him pull out in his Jeep. After the taillights disappear, I turn away and walk to the back of the house, on my way to the kitchen. As I pass the back door, something catches my eye, and I backtrack.

There's a red rose tied to the screen door with a black ribbon, something rolled up under the bow.

My stomach plummets, and I step onto the porch, pulling the rose off the handle with shaky hands. I glance around, half expecting to see someone watching, waiting. But I'm alone.

I unroll the photo, smoothing it out against my leg. As soon as I see what it is, though, I snatch my hand away like I've been burned, dropping the photo to the floor.

It's a photo of me, taken from a wide-angle lens. I'm standing next to my car, wearing the gray hoodie I wore a few days ago. Its fuzziness makes me wonder if it was taken from far away.

But there's nothing fuzzy about the meaning: someone really is watching me.

CHAPTER SEVENTEEN

Logan and I sit in politics the next day, side by side, as my stomach twists and turns. We're only a few minutes from walking down the hall to the other classroom to give our speeches. Mr. Patricks is currently writing the numbers one, two, and three on scraps of paper to determine our speech order.

As he drops the slips of paper into the bowl and walks up to Madison's desk, I rip out my own piece of paper and scribble down a note for Logan.

I found another rose.

Logan reads the note, then glances up, his eyes wide and concerned. He scribbles something down and slides it back.

Anything attached?

He pushes it in front of me, studying my expression as I read it.

Yeah. A photo of me. Like someone's following me. And I found the rose AT MY HOUSE.

I slide the note back, watching as Logan furrows his brow.

He doesn't seem to know what to say to this. I reach out, grab the paper, and scribble down, *Do you think it was Daemon?*

Logan reads the note, glancing up at me briefly, then writes, *He's not like that. He wouldn't go to all the effort.*

I slide the pen from his hand. *You didn't see how he was in the basement. Maybe you don't know him as well as you think you do.*

Logan reads the note, his eyes narrowed as he taps the pen on the desk, like he doesn't know what to write in response.

"I guess that just leaves one piece of paper," Mr. Patricks announces, jarring my focus back to him, where he's standing at the front of the class, holding up a scrap of paper. "Harper, you're the lucky winner. You'll give your speech first."

All thoughts of Daemon flee my mind as my stomach jumps into my throat. I think I might throw up.

"You can do this," Logan whispers.

I nod, fishing a stack of note cards out of my backpack.

"Okay guys, let's head down to room 203, shall we?"

My stomach lurches again as I get up and follow the trail of classmates into the hallway.

"You're going to do great," Logan says, coming up beside me. "You already faced two of your fears, right?"

I want to point out that neither occasion went smoothly, but I resist the urge.

Logan squeezes my arm. "Just read from the cards and glance up occasionally. We know our platform is more creative. There's no way it's not going to be more popular with the students. Just stick to what we rehearsed."

I nod, wishing it wasn't so hard to hear him over my thundering heart.

When we walk into room 203, I take in a deep, shaky breath. Lucas, Madison, and I walk to the front, where a long table with three chairs faces the class.

Half of my classmates end up seated on the floor or standing in the back, because there aren't enough chairs for everyone. Logan, meanwhile, manages to squeeze into the last empty chair near me and the other presenters.

I take the seat at the far right, next to Madison. She leans over, flashing me a smile that sends butterflies raging to life. "I can't wait to watch you humiliate yourself," she mutters.

Mr. Patricks walks to the front of the room, then turns to address the students. "Thank you, everyone, for accommodating us today. As you've probably heard, our first period politics class is running a mock election. Seated before you are our three candidates, and they are each here today to give you an outline of their campaigns. Please pay attention to their speeches. Soon, you will be given the opportunity to vote for one of these candidates."

Mr. Patrick turns to our table. "So without further ado, Harper, you may begin."

I gulp, shakily gathering my cards up as heat creeps into my cheeks.

Madison leans over, whispering under her breath, "Don't screw up."

When she sits back, her smile is cruel.

I look around the rest of the classroom, desperate to overcome the feeling that there's a hot spotlight shining down on me. Two dozen eyes stare back at me, watching me. And for one second, I forget where I am, thinking of something—of someone—else who seems to be watching me. I think of the roses. Of the pictures.

When my gaze lands on Logan, I push away all thoughts of the flowers from a would-be stalker. He smiles encouragingly and mouths, *You can do it.*

The strange thing is that as I stare into his eyes, I actually believe it. Then, before I know it, the first few words of my speech are out of my mouth. "Um, my name is Harper Bennett and I am running as an independent candidate."

I clear my throat and quickly glance down at my cards. "My platform is based around student life. And I can promise you that if I'm elected, your daily experiences as a student will improve."

My hands are visibly shaking, making it hard to read my cards. I force my fingers to release their death grip as I glance up at Logan. He's nodding encouragingly and it gives me a burst of confidence. "Washington State law provides for longer break times than EHS currently offers. If elected, I plan to campaign to increase our break times."

Someone in the back whoops, and I smile for the first time since I walked into the room. Beside me, Madison huffs under her breath, like the mere idea of someone rooting for me is ridiculous.

"Further, as your president, I would approach local restaurants such as Frankie's Pizza to discuss the idea of allowing them a space in our cafeteria. This would increase student options for lunch without costing the school district any money."

A few people in the back clap, and I meet Logan's eyes. *I told you so*, he mouths.

As I smile back at him, I realize he's right. Maybe this list of mine isn't just a list of fears. Maybe it *is* a to-do list.

And maybe with Logan's help, I can cross off each one.

CHAPTER EIGHTEEN

From the cracked vinyl driver's side seat of my battered old car, I lean across the console, arranging a couple of grocery bags on the passenger side floorboard. When the alarm of a nearby car chirps, I glance up. It's Logan, decked out in a track-suit and ball cap—stuff he never wears—walking toward me as he skirts a puddle. The rain pours down so hard he's hunched over, chin tucked into his jacket.

It only takes an instant to realize it's not Logan.

It's Daemon.

And even though I've been waiting to confront him, I can't help but shrink down in my seat, so that only the top of my head pokes over the window. I watch as Daemon climbs into a dark SUV—one that I think belongs to his uncle—just two spots away from me, slamming the door hard behind him.

He starts the car and backs it out of the stall, his headlights illuminating my car for a heart-stopping moment. I freeze, hoping he didn't see me, hoping the raindrops trickling down my window were enough to blur my face.

As Daemon pulls away, my eyes lock onto the oversized chrome grill on the front of the car. It's bent in the middle, caved in.

A wave of horror washes over me.

It was a dark SUV that hit Bick. The grill could be bent because he rammed into Bick's truck.

I sit upright, twisting the key in the ignition and sliding the car into drive. Without a second thought, I turn to follow Daemon, turning onto Roosevelt Avenue just as the light turns green.

My heart feels strange and fluttery, my nerves wound up, but I can't seem to stop myself from following him as he turns again, down a back road.

"Where are you going?" I mumble to myself. His house is on the opposite side of town, and as far as I know, he has no friends in Enumclaw. How would he make them when he's homeschooled?

I maintain a good quarter-mile between us as I follow him, my hands gripping the wheel so hard it's almost painful. As he pulls up to a four-way stop, he seems to accidently hit his brights, because they flash a moment before his blinker clicks on and he turns left.

I slow as he turns, and wait a moment longer at the four-way stop so that he'll get further ahead. I don't want to lose him, but I *really* don't want him to realize he's being followed.

While I'm waiting, I glance up at the stop sign, shining

under the lamplight, and realize it's new. The original must have been one of the ones that went missing.

I glance back down the street and decide it's safe to follow at this distance. Still, I wish we weren't the only ones on the road. It seems so glaringly obvious that I'm following him, but I can't seem to resist. Daemon's up to something, and I want to know what.

By the time he makes it to a second stop sign, I'm only a few hundred yards back. This time, I can see that he stops just shy of the sign and doesn't immediately flip on his blinker, just waits.

My stomach climbs into my throat. There are no turns between me and that sign. If I keep going, I'm going to come to a stop right behind him, bumper to bumper.

I glance at the locks on my door and wonder if I should just whip a U-turn rather than catch up with him.

But then he flashes his brights again, and the white-striping on the stop sign reflects the light. He flips on his right blinker and heads down the next road.

I pull to a stop next to the sign and stare up at it through the raindrops shimmering on my window. And that's when I realize it's a replacement sign, just like the other one. Even the pole is new.

Maybe flashing his lights wasn't an accident. . . . Maybe he's trying to show me something.

But that means he knows I'm following him. He must know who I am. Maybe he saw me in the parking lot.

Why is he doing this? Why is he showing me the signs?

Even though I know it's stupid—dangerous, even—I turn right and follow him again, hitting the gas to catch up. There's no point in playing dumb. He knows I'm here, and he'll probably just wait for me if I fall too far behind.

When Daemon flashes his lights and glides to a stop at the next sign, I don't have to wonder if the sign next to him is new.

Does this mean he's taking credit for removing the signs? Doesn't he know people got hurt—that it wasn't a silly prank?

As I follow him into the shadows behind Mount Peak, I remember the dented chrome grill, and fear creeps in. Bick says he was run off the road. Says the SUV rammed right into him, and then took off. The memory of the red handprint flashes in my head. The one on Bick's truck.

But then there was also the other one . . . the one left on my car door. The handprint that I thought was made of real blood. Somehow, while Bick helped me get paper towels, it disappeared. Was it Daemon who cleaned it off? Was he in the lot? Did he remove it so that I couldn't report it?

Then it hits me: What if Daemon is taking me down these backroads so that he can run me off the road?

I tighten my hands on the wheel as I realize my mistake. I shouldn't have followed him. I glance in my rearview mirror, trying to decide if I should just turn around. There aren't many houses directly behind me, but there are several just ahead, and from there I can turn left and drive closer to town.

But I don't end up having much of a choice. Daemon pulls over in a big gravel turnout, leaving his brights on full blast.

I slam on my brakes and watch him from where I sit, my car idling in the middle of the road. The only streetlight near me is burnt out, leaving the inside of my car pitch-black.

He flashes his lights into the tree line. Once, twice, three times. It seems deliberate, like he wants me to see something.

But what's he trying to show me?

Before I can figure it out, he slams down on the gas, and gravel shoots out from under his tires as he turns hard. The SUV whips around, and his brights shine right into my eyes.

I put a hand up to block the glare and realize with horror he's accelerating right at me.

My heart turns to a thunderous roar as I glance to my right and left, trying to figure out a way to go—a way to save myself from the five-thousand-pound vehicle barreling my way.

But it's too late.

I let out a strangled cry and throw my hands up to shield my face just as the SUV bears down, closes the gap to a foot . . .

But it doesn't hit me, it just roars right past, inches shy of my window.

Eyes wide, I watch the red taillights disappear in my rearview mirror as I gasp for air, try to bring the world back under control. I twist around in my seat and glance back, convinced that to him this is a game, that he's going to reappear at any moment.

But he doesn't.

My wipers screech on the windshield, and I realize the rain has stopped. I flip them off and stare at where my headlights illuminate the gravel turnout.

Curiosity overwhelms me. I pull forward, turn into the shoulder, and put my car in park, shutting off the engine. I climb out and walk to the road, listening for the sound of Daemon's car. But the night is silent.

I turn back to the gravel and follow the glare of my headlights, walking to the edge of the gravel.

Something is reflecting back at me in the darkness. I rest my good hand on the trunk and step forward, peering into the trees. As my eyes adjust, I realize what I'm looking at.

Stop signs.

CHAPTER NINETEEN

I'm sitting in the hay barn, breathing in the deep, sweet scent of the alfalfa to try to calm my nerves, when Logan's Jeep crosses the gravel driveway. He pulls right under the eave of the barn, turning the engine off.

I stand, wiping the hay from the seat of my jeans, and walk to him.

"Hey," he says, climbing out of his Jeep.

"Hi." My voice is curt. Short.

"So . . . what's up? Your texts were . . . mysterious." He smiles, but when he sees my flat stare, his expression changes. "Something wrong?"

"What the hell did Daemon do in Cedar Cove? And not the Cliff Notes version, the whole story."

Logan looks like I've slapped him. "What?"

"Was it criminal?" I ask, stepping closer.

His lips part, but he doesn't speak.

"I saw Daemon in town last night. I followed him."

Logan pales. "You shouldn't have done that."

I laugh, a humorless laugh. "Why? You haven't told me everything, have you? What are you hiding? Why are you protecting him?"

"It doesn't matter what he did," Logan says, his voice even. "That's behind us."

I stare him straight in the eyes, taking another step toward him. "Is it? Because my evening was rather . . . illuminating."

Logan swallows, but he doesn't speak as he meets my gaze.

"He's responsible for removing the stop signs, Logan. And I think he's the one who ran Bick off the road."

Logan's lips part, but he doesn't speak, just meets my gaze with fear and pain and dejection swirling in his eyes. He knows I'm right and he *still* won't admit it.

"You can't keep doing this. You have to stop covering for him," I say, my voice lower.

Logan shakes his head so hard I'm surprised his neck doesn't hurt. "It's not like that."

"No? Because it sure as hell seems like it. You had to have seen his car. Known it matched Bick's description. Noticed the enormous dent in the grill."

"It has a dent?" He pinches his nose, closing his eyes like he's trying hard to come to terms with this.

"Don't act like you didn't know," I snap.

He opens his eyes and gives me a hurt look. "I didn't. He parks it in the garage. You've been to my house. You would have seen it too."

I open my mouth to argue, but I can't. It's true. I've been

to Logan's house since Bick's accident and I didn't notice the dent either.

I walk away from Logan, plunking down on the hay bale and pulling out several stalks of alfalfa. "Tell me what he did before, Logan. I deserve to know."

"Please. I thought you understood," he says, making no move to follow me. "I just want to be with you. I want it to be about us. Not him."

"How can there be an us with him acting like he is? When I know you're keeping secrets? You know everything about me, but all I know about you—about him—is what you've told me." I twist the stalks together as I think of how he severed all ties with his old friends. He's hiding something. I just don't know what.

Or why.

"Is this the Spanish Inquisition?" He wants it to sound like a joke but it doesn't. It sounds defensive.

"No, but I need to know. Daemon's doing some scary things. Endangering people's lives. If I'm going to be with you . . . I need to know what we're dealing with."

"If?" he says, finally moving toward me and sitting down beside me. He reaches for my hand, but I pull it away. "Please don't tell me we just became an *if.*"

I push myself off the hay, whirling on him. "Daemon tried to kill one of my best friends!"

"You don't know that!" He groans, his face in his hands, his hair flopping into his eyes.

I cross my arms. "Then fill in the blanks, Logan. Tell me everything that happened in Cedar Cove."

DANGEROUS BOY

He doesn't answer.

I chew on my lip until it hurts, staring right at him, but he doesn't look up to meet my eyes. "You know what? Screw it. Keep your stupid secrets."

I stomp out of the barn and toward the house, my heart aching with the hope that Logan will follow. The hope he's going to offer me an explanation.

But pretty soon I'm all alone, and no explanation comes.

CHAPTER TWENTY

The next evening, I'm crouched down behind some shrub-
bery, halfway down Logan's driveway, when I hear a car
door slam, and then moments later, another. I hold my breath
as the engine fires up and the now-familiar SUV glides by.

The sight of the bent front grill makes any guilt I had for
what I'm about to do disappear. Every sign points to one explanation for why the grill is bent: Daemon wrecked Bick's
car. Deliberately. He's a danger to me, my friends, and the
whole town, and since Logan won't stop protecting him, I've
decided that it's up to me to get proof on my own.

I count to thirty, until the rumble of the engine disappears.
Then I stand up and walk down the tree-lined lane until the
house appears before me in all its classic, Victorian glory. It's
dark, eerie in the silent afternoon light.

I walk faster, staring up at the windows, waiting for any
sign of life. But the curtains are still, the lights off.

I go to the front door and ring the bell, then dash back to

hide behind a bush and wait. Their uncle is supposedly out of town and I heard two doors slam, so I'm fairly sure Logan and Daemon left together, but I have to be careful.

Nobody answers, so I slip around the house, to the back door. When Logan was driving the other day, I noticed that he doesn't have a house key dangling on his key ring. Either he doesn't need one, or they hide a key. And if they hide a key, I'm betting it's near the back door.

I slink around the back, sneaking along the shadows, and then stop near the back entry, surveying the gardens and the rocks, looking for anything out of place that might conceal a key. But nothing stands out.

So I pick up the mat and look under there. No dice.

As a last resort, I slide my fingers over the doorframe.

Bingo. A single key. It's old and rusty, and I can't help but wonder if the locks are the same ones that were there when the Carsons lived inside. I shrug off the thought and pop the key in. The door creaks as I push it open, causing me to cringe.

"Logan?" I call out, my voice pathetically shaky. I'm getting nervous, now, but I've come this far.

I step back and replace the key, and then enter the house, my feet whisper silent as I step down the dark hall. All I can hear is the pounding of my own heartbeat.

Daemon didn't give me a very extensive tour when I was here last—other than of the basement—but he did show me where the bedrooms are, so that's where I'll start.

The hardwood steps creak with each footstep. I pause in

the middle and listen again, but there's nothing but shadows and silence.

I make my way to the top of the stairs and go to the door directly across the hall. Logan told me the other day that the bedroom with the fluttering dark curtains belonged to Daemon, which makes it this bedroom.

One curtain is open, the last dying rays of sunlight streaming in. I creep up to the big dark teak antique dresser. When I open the top drawer, I'm disappointed to see nothing but socks. Undeterred, I dig around a bit, and my fingers slide across something hard.

I pull it out, shock surging through me as I realize what I'm holding.

A can of red paint. The same kind we were using to prepare for the Halloween Masquerade. It's light, mostly empty. I stare at it for a long moment, remembering the red handprints that emblazoned the car windows at school.

I blink away the image and put the can back where I found it. So the handprints were Daemon's, which means he *did* wreck Bick's car . . . unless he was seeking recognition for something he didn't actually do. That seems unlikely, especially because he also seemed to take credit for the stop signs.

I shudder. How can Logan ignore this? He must know. He has to.

I rifle through the other drawers, uncovering little more than track pants, ball caps, and soccer shirts. I go to the closet and pull open the double doors, but inside it's mostly empty. A jacket, two pairs of sneakers, and a few discarded books.

I'm not sure what I'd expected. Newspaper clippings? This all looks so easy on *CSI*.

Maybe it's Logan who keeps the sentimental things. He has the photo album, after all. He might have kept some other mementoes of their time in Cedar Cove.

I stop at the entrance to Daemon's room and look to my right, to the door that belongs to their uncle's room, or at least that's what Daemon claimed. So I go left, to the third door, where I think I'll find Logan's room.

The floor creaks under my feet as I approach his room. Just as my fingers touch the solid wood five-paneled door, I hear something.

Tires on gravel.

My heart leaps to my throat and I rush back to the window in Daemon's room, where I look out to see the dark SUV rolling down the driveway.

Great. They must have forgotten something. I rush back into the hall, giving one last longing glance at Logan's room. I need to explore it. I need to know what secrets he and his brother are hiding.

Now I won't have the chance.

I scramble down the stairs, my fingers gliding down the wooden banister. I can't be caught in here. Logan can't know.

I fly out the back door, barely stopping to close it behind me, and across the back lawn. I hear a car door slam shut as I sprint across the grass and dash into the tree line.

I go down almost immediately, tripping on a tree root I

didn't see in the shadows. I lie there on the ground for a long moment, staring up into the cloudy sky, catching my breath as the painful throbbing in my shoulder recedes. At the rate I'm going, my collarbone is never going to heal.

I listen until the back door of the house squeaks open and bangs shut, and then I get up and run, weaving in and out of the trees, until I'm around the front of the house.

And then I race down the driveway and out onto the main road, to where my car's hidden around the corner, my heart thundering in my ears until I'm safely ensconced inside.

Daemon stole stop signs. Put blood-red handprints on my car and dozens of others. He must have left me the roses with the twisted notes and messed with the wheel on the quad. Who knows if he had anything to do with the cow bones and dead birds? And he nearly killed Bick.

How far will he go if I don't stop him?

CHAPTER TWENTY-ONE

"How do you feel about a road trip?" I ask, sliding into the passenger seat of Adam's Samurai. I asked him to pick me up this morning, but I never told him why his services were required.

Come to think of it, there's actually a slim chance Logan will show up around ten minutes from now to find that I've already left, but it serves him right for keeping secrets.

Adam blinks. He doesn't even look fully awake yet. "Um, to where?"

I purse my lips. "Oregon."

"And why, exactly, do we need to ditch class and drive three hours?" he asks, his brows scrunched up. "Besides, I'm supposed to help Allie bring a bunch of masquerade stuff to the gym this morning. You know, because I'm such a strong guy and all."

I ignore his lame attempt at a joke. "I want to go to Cedar Cove."

He narrows his eyes. "Isn't that—"

"It's where Logan's from."

Adam frowns. "Look, I'm not taking you two on some—"

"He's not invited."

Adam scrunches his eyebrows together. "Care to explain?"

"There's something going on with his brother. Something that he's hiding from me. And I've gotta figure out what it is." I turn to Adam and put my hands up in a mock prayer. "Please, please, please, please? You know how I am about freeways. If you don't drive, I'll never get there."

"If Logan won't tell you anything, what makes you think—"

"People talk. There has to be somebody who knows what happened. Or school newspapers that would pick up stuff the regular media didn't."

"This is a little too Nancy Drew, don't you think? Maybe you should just leave it alone. Or better yet, just *ask* Logan."

I shake my head. "I *have* asked him, but he's too busy protecting his brother to tell me everything. Weird crap keeps happening, to me and half this town. I know it's bothering you too. This is our chance to figure it out."

Adam looks away, out the window. Which means he's thinking about it.

I chew on my lip, contemplating how much to reveal. "Look, I haven't told this to Bick, and I don't know if we should, because you know how he is. He'll take matters into his own hands. But I think Daemon's the one who wrecked him. I think Daemon's . . . activities started back when they were in

Cedar Cove. So I want to go down there and see if I can dig up anything. If we get enough evidence, we can go to the police. We have to stop him."

"Whoa, back up," Adam says, his eyes wide. "Why would Daemon go after Bick?"

"I don't know, and I have no proof."

I don't tell Adam about the paint can I found in Daemon's room. I can't exactly tell the cops I broke into his house and found it. And besides, Bick and I removed the red handprint from his truck. There's no longer anything to tie it to the accident.

"Please? I need you."

Adam sighs, shifting into gear. "All right, fine. Let's go."

The last hour of the drive to Cedar Cove takes us along a winding highway that threads through the foothills, bringing us closer to the Pacific Ocean with each shadowed bend and turn. A dark, oppressive cloud hangs low overhead, threatening rain.

When the road finally flattens out, adorable little motels and inns begin to dot the landscape, and that's how I know we're close. Billboards, seemingly out of place on such a quiet, rural road, crop up on each side, advertising suites and windsurfing and everything you'd expect from a coastal tourist trap.

Just past a sign for Go Karts and Putt-Putt golf, we pull onto the main drag and Adam stops at a red light. "So, what's the plan?" He glances at his watch. It's twelve forty already. The drive took even longer than I was expecting, especially since

Adam insisted on stopping for snacks. Twice. The wrappers litter the floorboards and a Big Gulp cup sits in the cup holder next to me.

I sit up in my seat. "Let's go to the school first. If we're lucky, it's big enough that we can slip in unnoticed," I say, pretending as if I know exactly where to start. It seemed obvious when we were in Enumclaw, but now that I'm here, I am not sure what to do. I find it difficult to believe that no one will notice the new girl with the shoulder brace.

"I don't know . . ." Adam says. "I don't think I want to trespass on school property."

I decide to take charge. "I just need to get into the library. And maybe talk to a few students, see if they remember Logan or Daemon."

Adam knows me too well to buy it. "Yeah, but it seems kinda sketchy," he says, flicking on his blinker and following the signs to the high school, despite his protest. "I'm not big on criminal records."

His words send a new wave of butterflies through my stomach, and I almost balk. It can't be criminal to walk around a high school if you're actually a teen, can it? It's not like we're planning to vandalize it or something.

Besides, I have to know what Logan is hiding. I have to know if the stuff that's happening to me—to the town—happened here. "Come on, it's not that big of a deal," I say, shrugging as if I actually believe that it's not. "We'll be there twenty minutes. Tops."

"Do I have to?" he asks.

"Did you see Bick's face?" I ask.

"Yeah," Adam says.

"Not the day it happened. You saw it a couple days later when he came back to class, and the swelling went down. He looked like he lost a fight with a brick wall the day I picked him up from the hospital."

Adam groans as he turns into the packed school parking lot, snagging one of the last available parking spaces at the back. "Okay, okay. You're right. Let's just get this over with."

I look around as he straightens out the car. I want people to think we're students, but I don't want to get caught by a school security guard who thinks we really *are* students, playing hooky. There's no way I can explain to my dad why I'm five hours away in the principal's office at the wrong high school. I'd be lucky if he remembers Logan's name, let alone understands why I'm all the way down here, investigating his past.

"Come on," I say. We get out of the car and walk to the side doors while Adam shoves his keys into his pocket. I glance around, taking it all in as I bury my hands in the front pocket of my hoodie. An ocean breeze, briny and fresh, drifts over us. The school is not very big, a little smaller than Enumclaw, probably has a couple hundred students in each class. Hopefully the size helps. If it were too big, there'd always be the chance that people wouldn't remember Logan, but if it were too small, everyone would know we don't belong here.

It's pretty, though, with a manicured lawn and hedges, and it's made of brick, with a glass sculpture meant to mimic ocean waves sweeping across the wall near the main entrance.

We step into the halls just as a shrill bell rings out, and in an instant, we're jammed into a mix of students, shoulder-to-shoulder. Adam grabs my elbow, linking us together as we push through the crowd.

I see a giant sign proclaiming MAIN OFFICE and move faster, dragging Adam behind me even as I knock into student after student. We might not be low profile, but I don't want anyone from the school administration seeing me, knowing I don't belong.

We round the corner and my heart thump-thumps when I see a placard for the library hanging from the breezeway. We scurry across the courtyard, our feet nearly silent on the concrete. I tighten my grip on Adam's hand and pull him harder, wanting this mission to be over, wanting to get to the truth and just . . . *know.* We step into the library, the sounds of the crowd dying instantly. A few students look up at us, curious, and I hope I'm right—I hope this school is big enough that we seem anonymous.

"Come on," I say, faking confidence, control. "I want to see if there are any student newspapers from the time Logan was here."

Adam shrugs and follows me, having given up any further attempts at protest. We weave between tables sparsely populated with students quietly studying and eating lunch, toward a circular desk in the back.

"Excuse me," I say, stepping up to the guy behind the desk. Huh. I don't know that I've ever seen a guy school librarian before. I can't decide if this is a good thing or a bad thing. I was hoping for a sleepy, detached sort of librarian. "I'm looking for the student papers from last spring and fall. Do you know where I can find them?"

"Yeah, they'd be on microfiche," he says, pointing to the machine across the room. "We don't switch to digital until we get the new computer system in next year. Gray cabinet next to it houses the film. Most recent in the front of the top drawer, so last spring would only be a couple folders back. Copies are ten cents each. Pick up your prints here."

I nod, turning away. Perfect.

"Haven't seen you in here before," he says, eyeballing me. I swallow.

"Yeah, um, usually I eat lunch with my, um, boyfriend." I nod in Adam's direction, trying not to grimace at the mere idea of Adam being my boyfriend. Ick. I should have convinced Bick to come down here instead; at least that'd almost be believable. Then again, he still has faint, fading bruises on his face, so maybe we'd look more suspicious. "But, see, we have a bet going. About, uh, who was prom queen last year."

The librarian gives us this half-bored, half-annoyed look, as if to say *kids these days.*

"Anyway, thanks!"

I spin around and walk away as slowly as my legs will allow. "That was close," I mutter to Adam. "I thought he was going to ask us for student ID or something."

"Miss!" the guy calls out, and I freeze, my lungs stuck somewhere in my throat as I turn back around. "You forgot this," he says, holding up the pen I'd been tapping on his counter.

"Oh, uh, thanks." I scurry back, grab it, and then rejoin Adam over by the microfiche. I don't even think it's my pen, but I am not about to argue and raise more questions.

"Remind me to never let you become a secret agent," Adam says, shaking his head. "That was terrible."

"Whatever," I say, opening up the gray cabinet next to the microfiche machine. "I can't even believe they still use one of these things."

"Old habits die hard?"

"I guess so."

I gather the seven folders that cover the previous school year.

"What are you looking for, exactly?" Adam asks, sliding another chair over as I settle down in front of the machine.

"I don't know yet. I guess I'll know it when I see it."

"Well, you'd better hurry."

I shuffle through the film, glancing up at him. "Why? It's not like we're going to make it back to EHS in time. We have all day."

He glances up at the clock. "Not if we're students here. Unless you want our cover blown, we probably have twenty minutes. Whenever that bell rings, we need to leave for our supposed classes."

His warning sends a wave of nerves through me. Somehow I'd forgotten that fact. "Good thing you're here," I say.

Adam smiles ruefully and turns to the screen as I slide the first bit of film onto the panel.

"It's upside down and backward," he says.

"Obviously. It's not like I've even used one of these things before. It's prehistoric." I slide the film out and invert it, then push it back in.

Cedar Cove Buzz emblazons the screen. A handful of articles about an upcoming student election, prom ticket prices, and changes to the cafeteria menu greet me. My eyes search every corner of the film, but there's nothing out of the ordinary. I rein in my worry and slide the sheet out, setting it next to the machine.

"Next," I say, holding my hand out.

He slaps a new sheet of film down and I stick it into the machine, my heart plummeting as I see the first headline, then scan the rest of the page. All it's got is as an article about the Mathletes' returning senior members, an op-ed about the aging coaching staff, and a student-written poem.

I deflate. *Please don't let this whole thing be for nothing. Five hours in the car, the assignments I'm going to have to do for Adam, skipping school . . . all to dig into Logan's past. Logan, my boyfriend.*

But I know I'm on to something. I can practically feel it, dangling just out of my reach. I can't stop until I know what happened here. Logan and Daemon fled this town for a reason. If I can uncover it, I'll know why he lied about Daemon.

"Next," I say.

Ten minutes later, I'm growing panicky. We have to pack up soon and I have nothing. The next sheet has something about the semester's standardized testing and another stupid cafeteria menu.

"Next," I say. We're almost a full year back now, to last fall.

I slide the black-and-white page into the screen and my heart slams into my throat as the picture comes into focus.

Logan's face greets me.

"So, there he is," I announce. "We found him." I look over at Adam, trying to steel my nerves for whatever this story is going to say.

But his expression is one of confusion. "Uh, Harper, not exactly."

"What?"

"Look at the headline," he replies, his voice as hard as stone.

I look down slowly and that's when I see it. Above Logan's picture. I can't bring myself to read it aloud.

Adam does it for me. "Student *Trent Townsend* paints the sophomore homecoming float," he says, slowly, deliberately, as if he's even more baffled than I am. His jaw drops, and he turns to stare at me.

We fall silent. I'm frozen, staring at Logan's face, grainy in black and white as my fingers tremble against the microfiche machine.

"So one of them is really named Trent," Adam finally says.

I turn to him. "The question is, which one?"

CHAPTER TWENTY-TWO

slam the passenger door to Adam's car, on the verge of tears. One way or another, Logan lied.

Again.

"So, do you think it's Logan or Daemon who is really Trent?" Adam asks, trying to get me to do more than just sit there dejectedly in my seat.

"I dunno," I respond. It's too hard to think. I feel sick to my stomach.

Adam pats me on the shoulder. "Well, my guess is that since Logan's actually enrolled in school, he probably had to use his real name, so it's probably Daemon who is Trent."

I bet that's true. He couldn't be at Enumclaw using a false name, could he?

Adam stares out the windshield, chewing on his lip. At least he's on board with my investigation now, instead of acting like it's stupid. "Have you tried to Google Daemon's name?"

"Yeah. And I got nothing," I say, unable to even fake a

neutral voice. "Absolutely nothing." I'm crushed and embarrassed and confused, and I feel so entirely pathetic I just want to crawl into the backseat of the Samurai and curl up with a blanket over my head for the rest of the day.

"Not even a Facebook page, an old news story, Twitter?"

I shake my head. "No. Logan's got a Facebook page, but Daemon doesn't. Unless he's Trent . . . *Oh*," I say, finally getting what Adam's saying. "If his real name is Trent, I wouldn't find anything under Daemon."

Adam chews on his lip and stares out the windshield. "So that means the picture of 'Trent,'" he says, using air quotes, "is probably 'Daemon,'" he says, using the air quotes again.

"Yeah." I slide further into my seat, propping my knees up on the dashboard. "How did I get to this point? That I'm playing private investigator on my own boyfriend?"

Adam shrugs. "I dunno. Can't say I saw it coming myself." Adam gives me *the look*. "And if you can't trust him, what's the point?"

"I don't know. I just feel different around him. He *gets* me." I frown, blinking away the threat of tears. "It probably doesn't even matter. I told him off on Friday and we haven't talked since."

"It's probably for the best," Adam says, in his softest voice. I wonder if he can actually hear my heart breaking.

I swallow, but it does nothing about the lump in my throat. "Maybe he has a really good reason for all this."

"Don't you think if he had one, he would have offered it up by now? It's all more than a little suspicious."

I sigh deeply and turn back to the window.

Turns out that driving to Cedar Cove didn't give me any answers.

Just a whole new set of questions.

Back at home, I slide my laptop across my bed. I burrow into my thick comforter, lean back on a few pillows, and click the computer on.

Dad's still outside, fighting the falling darkness to finish the green-chop, gathering up grass to bring in and feed the cows. It's time consuming but he does it every chance he gets. The grass in the field is free. The alfalfa truck is not.

Maybe we can't afford to just buy hay all the time or hire a bunch of help, but I wish my dad would just take an afternoon off somehow. Come inside and watch a movie with me. Ask me how my day was.

Act like I exist. After he had such a strong reaction at the hospital when I broke my collarbone, I kind of thought it might be a wake-up call. But it wasn't. He didn't even stay until I was done, and by the time Logan brought me home, he was working out in the barns.

My computer finally boots up and I pop open Google, input *Trent Townsend*, and sit back, my stomach in my throat as I hit "enter" with shaky fingers. As my computer fetches the results, I close my eyes.

I want to know, but then again I don't. I have this overwhelming feeling that I'm standing at the edge of a cliff, about to jump.

I open my eyes, and my vision swims with headlines.

CEDAR COVE STUDENT EXPELLED FOR HARASSMENT

CEDAR COVE TEEN CHARGED WITH ASSAULT

CEDAR COVE HIGH THE EPICENTER OF VIOLENCE?

I think I'm going to be sick. My room spins around me as I stare at the monitor, my fingers trembling on the keyboard. I'm afraid to click on anything. I'm staring for so long, in the growing darkness, that my phone ringing terrifies me so much I leap into the air, narrowly saving my laptop from flying across the room.

Willing my racing heart back under control, I reach for my cell.

Adam.

I click it on and put it to my ear, wondering belatedly if my heartbeat will be heard over the phone.

"I don't want you talking to him," Adam says.

"Did you—"

"Trent Townsend, Google result number six. Click it."

I pull my computer back onto my lap and push the screen back. With a shaky hand, I click on number six.

> In a scene reminiscent of a bad B movie, a party turned violent last Saturday for several Cedar Cove High students. Among them was Trent Townsend, a student who is now accused of assault on Cedar Cove's quarterback in what many believe was a case of rivalry over a girl. Saturday's party escalated, leaving two students in the hospital . . .

"I can't read it," I choke out.

"I'm coming over," Adam says. I can hear him moving around, like he's throwing on his shoes or a jacket or something.

"No, don't do that. I'm fine," I say. "I just need time to sit and think."

"What is there to think about?" Adam asks. "The guy is fucked up. You're probably right and he did run Bick off the road—"

"You can't tell him that," I interrupt. "Bick would fly over there in a second to confront him, and you know that wouldn't end well."

"What are we supposed to do with all this? We know he's dangerous. We can't just sit around and ignore it. What about the roses, Harper? He's targeting you too."

I nod, the lump in my throat rendering me unable to speak. "I know—"

"I'm picking you up in the morning," Adam says. "We'll figure out how to keep you safe. We're probably going to have to go to the cops." He pauses. "You should tell your dad."

I close my eyes and pinch the bridge of my nose. "Fine. Whatever."

"I'm serious. He needs to know what's going on with you. And if you get any more roses or notes, don't touch them. Put them in plastic bags or something. We might want to give them to the police."

Suddenly I just want this conversation to be over. "Okay, okay. My dad's out doing the green-chop but I'll tell him in the morning."

"I know you think I'm overreacting, but I just want to be sure nothing happens to you. So promise me you won't leave the house without me."

"Okay. Okay. I promise."

I click the phone off and slide deeper into the blankets. I pull the thick quilt up to my chin and then curl in around my pillow, willing the gaping black hole in my stomach to go away.

How much of what Logan's told me has just been a bunch of bull? Even when he told me about Daemon, he lied. He gave me a false name so I wouldn't know the full extent of what had happened in Cedar Cove. Why didn't he tell me what *really* happened? Why's he so desperate to hide the truth about his brother?

The first tears brim, sliding down my temple and dampening my pillow. I cry silently, choking back sobs. I thought I didn't believe in love. But then I met Logan, and for a moment, lived in Allie's fantasy world of happily ever after and sunshine and rainbows.

I thought I would have that, with Logan.

And now I'm not even sure that's his real name.

CHAPTER TWENTY-THREE

The next morning, I sit in Adam's car at the curb near the school.

At least I talked him into parking a block away, so that I could put off this day for just a moment longer. I need time to figure out what I plan to say to Logan when he walks into politics.

Today's our last day of campaigning, but we still have posters to put up. It's going to be so hard to work with him when I feel like such an emotional mess.

"I called Bick last night," Adam says, his voice hesitant.

I whip around. "What did you tell him?"

Adam slides his phone shut. "I didn't tell him we think it's Daemon who wrecked his car. You're right about that: he can't know. But I told him to meet us in the morning. I just texted him to tell him where we're parked."

"Why?"

"Because I want his help watching Logan," he says, tapping his fingers on the steering wheel.

"And what's he going to do? Put on a bulletproof vest and interrogate him? Jesus, you're acting like he's a wanted murderer." I grip the door handle, wanting to just jump out and go for a long walk somewhere until my head clears and I can puzzle out all these pieces, figure out what to do next.

"We don't know *who* he is. All we know is he didn't tell you about anyone named Trent, or what happened at his old school. And we *do* know you've received threats on campus. Bick needed to know. I can't just watch you by myself."

"I am *not* telling Bick what's going on."

"Goddamn it, Harper. Why do you always have to be so difficult? It's okay to need help." Adam punches his steering wheel and the horn lets out a little chirp. "I'm not taking no for an answer. Until we know what we're dealing with, someone is going to be around you at all times."

"You're overreacting. Logan's never said or done—"

"Let's recap, shall we? He tried to cover up his brother's existence, and then he gave you a false name. His brother seemed threatening when you met him at the house, and then you discovered he's responsible for removing the stop signs. We also think he ran Bick off the road. Meanwhile, weird shit has been happening all over town, you've received roses with threatening poems and pictures with your eyes blacked out, and you got injured on a sabotaged quad. I'm not overreacting, and I swear to God if you say that one more time—"

"I get it, Adam."

"I was up half the night reading all those articles," he says, his voice softer now, less angry. "There was a girl. She got hurt."

"How?"

"I don't know. But something went on, you know it as well as I do, and"—Adam's voice breaks—"and you need to be cautious." He stares at the steering wheel, his finger tracing the Suzuki symbol.

"Adam—"

A rap on the window makes me jump nearly out of my chair, my heart exploding in my chest.

Bick. It's just Bick.

"Jesus, Adam, how about you don't get me so freaked out I leap into the air?" I glare at him.

Adam shrugs, then opens his window to let Bick lean in.

"Mornin'," Bick calls, resting his forearms on the window-sill. "What's going on? You're being all secretive and shit."

Bick, always a way with words.

"Adam's needlessly pretending like he's my big bro," I say, glaring. "Nothing new there."

Adam shakes his head. "Not-uh, Harper. You tell him or I will."

I roll my eyes and grit my teeth. "Turns out Logan's twin brother may have done some illegal—"

"Violent," Adam interrupts.

"May have done some illegal, *possibly violent* things in the past."

"No shit?" Bick's eyes are wide, and he scratches at his goatee. "Why have I never met this guy, anyway?"

I sigh. This is going exactly like I thought it would. "He's homeschooled."

Adam rolls his eyes. "And why is that, Harper?"

"Because he was expelled from his last school," I mumble.

Adam takes that as his cue to lay all the cards on the table. "And Logan's being less than truthful, so we don't actually know the extent of things. Until further notice, we're sticking to Harper like glue."

Allie's going to be thrilled when I monopolize all her time with Adam . . .

Adam continues, "I've got first period at the opposite end of campus, and you're two doors down, so you're hereby her morning escort."

"You don't think—" Bick starts.

"No, I don't think I'm in mortal peril," I say, shooting another look at Adam. "Adam just watches too many movies. Can we go now?"

Adam turns to Bick. "You got it?"

"Sure. If I lose sight of her, do I get a fog horn or something?" he says, grinning.

Adam rolls his eyes again and looks like he's going to say something more, but another glare from me silences him.

"Come on, we're going to be late." I yank my backpack off the floorboards and throw it over my good shoulder, following Bick's bulky frame across the street, still fuming. We're through the double-glass doors before Adam has even zipped up his backpack and locked his Samurai.

We take a left toward the English and history wing, making our way to my politics class. Just outside the classroom, Bick stops and turns to me. In the fluorescent lighting of the school halls, I can still see a yellowish tinge under his eye, a lingering sign of his accident. "You sure you're cool?" he asks.

I nod. "Adam's totally overblowing this whole thing. Logan's never done anything to hurt me. It's his brother."

"That's what I figured." Bick grins at me, but then his smile fades, and he no longer looks quite so at ease. I know without looking up that Bick's wary expression means Logan is approaching.

"Hey," Logan says, his voice tentative. I glance over at him, take in the slump of his shoulders, and then turn back to Bick.

"Catch up with you later?" I ask.

Bick nods. "Yeah. Meet me here when class is over so we can, uh, talk about . . . that math test."

I grin despite myself. "Sure. Later." Bick is a really bad liar.

I watch as Bick walks away, and then turn to Logan, giving him a blank look. I hope the emotions swirling in my stomach aren't reflected in my eyes.

"So, um," Logan starts, staring down at his shoes. He sighs and finally meets my eyes. "Are you talking to me now?"

"I don't think so," I say, turning toward the classroom door. It's not that I think he's dangerous. Not in the literal sense. I trust *him* not to hurt me.

But he's allowing Daemon to hurt other people. He's standing by and staying silent, and he can't do that.

He follows me into the classroom. "I didn't mean to upset you," he says, plunking down in his chair.

"I know," I snap. "You also don't mean to tell me the truth."

He looks like he wants to say something, but Mr. Patricks chooses that moment to start class. "Okay guys, voting is this week, so you've got this period to make those last connections with your voter base. If you have any final posters to put up, you'll want to get that done today."

Logan and I stand without speaking, going to the back of the room where the four posters we made last week are sitting, stacked up on a table, next to at least twenty with VOTE FOR MADISON! written in glittery bubble letters. I want to shove them onto the dirty floor, just to let out my frustration at everything going on.

Logan picks up our posters and I follow him to the door, the silence between us stifling. We walk to the senior hall, and he sets the stack down on a window bay.

Logan holds up the first poster, and I lean over, pulling a piece of tape from the dispenser and pressing it to the corner of the cardstock. Logan scoots over to the other side, and I'm hyper-aware of his clean, soapy scent. It makes me want to drop the tape dispenser and just lean in to him, let him wrap his arms around me and tell me everything's going to be okay.

But the tension between us is palpable, and even if I wanted to make amends, I wouldn't know where to begin.

Fortunately, Logan makes the first move. "Are we going to talk about this?" he finally asks, as we're hanging our third poster.

"I'm not the one who needs to do the talking," I say, staring at the tape dispenser.

"You don't understand," Logan says.

"Then make me understand," I snap, turning to glare at him.

What if Adam's right? What if it was about a girl? What if Logan's brother has a problem with him being with me, and that's what the roses and notes are about? What if he stalks him, or me, and doesn't like seeing us together?

"He's . . . he's not me, Harper. He's not. It doesn't matter what he does, who he is. You're with me, and I never did anything wrong."

"You lied. About a lot of things. And right now? That's kind of all that matters. So when you're *really* ready to talk, let me know."

I push the last piece of tape onto the poster and then, without waiting for a response, I turn away and walk down the empty hallway.

Alone.

CHAPTER TWENTY-FOUR

On Friday, I'm sitting in a group of six, counting ballots. Logan is across the room, seated with five other students, a pile of ballots in front of him as well. To my relief, Mr. Patricks divided us all up so that we wouldn't be able to cheat in our calculations. I don't think I could have handled another minute of sitting so close to Logan with everything going on between us.

Each stack of ballots is double-counted, and then counted again if there are any discrepancies. I have a pile of ballots in front of me, and a pen in my hand. I unfold a scrap of yellow paper, and when I see *Harper Bennett* written inside, I add another tick to my column.

Madison, seated next to me, sort of growls under her breath as she takes the ballot and marks down another vote on her own sheet of paper.

I'm winning.

"You must have stuffed the box," Madison grumbles under her breath.

I roll my eyes. "Maybe my campaign was just better."

"Your campaign was not better. Your posters were stupid and your platform would never work in the real world. You're just lucky Mr. Patricks let it slide."

"Why do you hate me so much?" I ask.

Madison unfolds the ballot, and *Harper Bennett* is written in dark blue ink. "Do I need a reason?"

"Whatever," I say. At least with how things are with Logan, I won't be going to the masquerade tonight. I don't want to see Madison a moment more than absolutely necessary.

I open another ballot. *Madison Vaughn* is written inside. Of course. I push it onto her desk.

"You know, Logan's going to get tired of you, and then he'll want to see what being with a *real* girl is like. You're nothing but a boring loser."

My jaw drops but Madison ignores me, shoving her chair back as I unfold the final ballot and see my name staring back at me.

Madison disappears with the hall pass as I tally the final votes.

I've won by a landslide.

At home that night, I sit miserably in my room, listening to the pitter-patter of the rain. Dad's not home—whether he's at the vet or the feed store or a thousand other places, I don't know.

I used to go on errands with him. I'd sit on that wide bench seat in his truck, watching the world stream by. I wonder why

I stopped doing that. When the distance between us became more of a chasm.

The Halloween Masquerade starts in twenty minutes and my costume is hanging in my closet, still wrapped up in plastic. I sit curled up on the edge of my bed, leaning against the window, my forehead resting on the glass.

All those stupid decorations I made, and I'm not even going.

Logan acted like he was going to eat lunch with us like usual today, but I guess he got the hint when he walked up and I was seated between Adam and Bick, with Allie directly across from me, and there was no room for him. He stood there holding his tray for an agonizing moment, and then simply congratulated me on winning the election and turned on his heel, stalking away.

I wanted to say something to him—it was only because of him I even ran, and somehow it felt like I owed him some expression of gratitude, but I couldn't find the words.

This separation hurts unlike anything I could have imagined, and there's nothing I can do to change it. Apparently, keeping his secrets about Cedar Cove is worth the price of losing me.

Maybe it doesn't even matter. Daemon's proven to me he's dangerous. Being with Logan just puts me closer to that. I lean back against the window casing, cradling my arm in my lap. Below me, raindrops ripple across the surface of the mud puddles as the clouds darken.

This has been the worst streak of bad weather I can remember. I'm still sitting there, my temple resting on the cool glass, when a familiar red Jeep glides into the driveway.

Logan.

I'm so caught off guard, I don't move. I just stare down as he pulls to a stop and steps out, holding what appears to be a suit jacket over his head as he dashes to the back door, rapping hard on the screen.

I reluctantly uncoil from my spot near the window and go downstairs, my heart up in my throat as I open the door. Logan steps onto the darkened porch and follows me inside, and in the bright light of the kitchen, I realize he's wearing his costume.

It's a black tuxedo, shiny dress shoes and all, coupled together with a white mask that only covers one side of his face.

We were supposed to go as the couple from *The Phantom of the Opera*. He looks devastatingly handsome dressed as Erik, his eyes like dark orbs, one behind the mask, one uncovered.

"You can't think I'm still going," I say, taking in his rain-darkened hair.

He fiddles with a button on his tux, then looks up at me. "Look, I know I have no right to be standing here right now, but this week has been hell. I *need* you."

I cross my arms, as if it'll shield my heart. "So?"

He steps further into the house, taking small, tentative steps. When he looks up at me, I realize his eyes are red-rimmed, anguished. "And so I'm ready to talk. Come to the dance with me. I'll tell you everything you want to know on the way there, and if you want nothing to do with me after that, you can get a ride home from Allie or someone."

I swallow. I don't know how I'm supposed to talk to him with a lump this big in my throat.

"Okay. Fine. Give me five minutes. And then you can start with who the hell Trent Townsend is."

"Google is an interesting thing when you have the right name to search," I say, my voice bitter as I settle into the passenger seat of Logan's Jeep, arranging the full skirts of my old-fashioned dress. I'm wearing a big brunette wig, too. The curls cascade down my shoulders and end near my waist.

I left my brace at home. I'm supposed to wear it twenty-four-seven, but I think I can manage a few hours without it. I just couldn't ruin the effect of the dress with such an ugly scrap of fabric and Velcro.

Logan lets out a heavy sigh. "It's really coming down, isn't it?"

"*Logan.*" I snap. "Stop stalling and just tell me the truth already."

He swallows. "I guess you've figured it out anyway. Trent is his first name; Daemon is his middle name. He needed a fresh start. We agreed he'd go by Daemon."

"A fresh start from what? Or from *which* thing, should I say? That was some pretty heavy stuff that happened in Cedar Cove."

He nods, his lips pursed, his eyes turned downward. "I know."

"And you didn't think I deserved to be told?"

"Of course I did." He shakes his head, meeting my gaze

with glittering eyes. Somehow, it's like he's just as hurt as I am. "I just didn't want you to look at me like you are right now. Like you're disgusted by me. I didn't do those things, but everyone treats me as if I did."

"It's not what he did, Logan. It's what *you* did. How can I possibly be with you if I can't trust you to tell me the truth?"

He stares out into space as he pushes the key into the ignition and fires up the Jeep. "Please, Harper, just let me tell you everything, and then you decide what to do with it, okay?"

"Fine. Just don't leave anything out." I glare at him, awaiting the sordid details.

He nods, and the eye behind his mask is dark, shadowed and unreadable, while his other eye catches the glow of passing street lamps. The two, in combination, are an odd sort of contrast: night and day.

We pull out of the gravel driveway, turning right. Silence falls around us as we leave my house behind.

Then, suddenly, Logan speaks. "I was dating this girl, Deanna."

I swallow. Deanna. The brunette in the slinky dress on Facebook. I turn away from him to look out at the sparkling wet concrete.

"She was nice, into sports. We had that in common. We weren't really serious, but we were having fun, you know? But Trent kept screwing it up for me. Just like he is with you."

"Okay . . ."

"He went to school with me then, so it was harder. He'd

flirt with her, and make her uncomfortable. He couldn't get why she wouldn't go for him, even though he knew we were together."

"'Kay," I say, waiting for the story to take a turn for the worse.

"In a way, I think her attitude toward him reminded him of everything our dad did, and that's what really set him off. He's really weird about if someone favors me over him. He gets a little crazy."

That would have been good to know a few weeks ago. How could he know all this and not tell me? Warn me?

"Well, we were all three at this party. A big post-prom thing."

I blink, remembering the Facebook pictures, the pretty brunette. Were those newspaper stories—the ones about the fight at the party—about a post-prom party? Logan's staring straight ahead, at the road, and it's hard to see the expression in his dark eyes.

"I went with Deanna and some other couples, and we were having a great time. I went to the bathroom and when I came back, he was standing really close to her. I told him to back off and we got into an argument. Really escalated, turned physical. One of my buddies tried to jump in and help me and ended up getting hit in the face with a brass lamp. Broke his nose."

That doesn't sound like the news made it sound. It was just a fight at a high school party. Don't those happen all the time?

"And?"

He breathes deeply, staring out into the darkness as if lost in thought.

"Logan . . ." I coax, waiting for the rest of the story. Dying to know and . . . not wanting to hear it at the same time.

"So everyone tells him he has to leave, and he's over in the foyer, getting his shoes on. That's when I realize this girl is acting really weird."

My mouth goes dry. "Weird, like how?"

"Like, insanely drunk, even though I knew she'd only had one or two. She was leaning on me, her eyes kept half-closing even when she was talking. Her words were so slurred I couldn't really understand her. I had to hold her up."

"So what, she was slamming shots when no one was looking?"

Logan shakes his head but he won't look at me, just keeps staring at the road. Finally, he breaks the silence. "No. It was him."

I open my mouth to speak, but the words don't come. I think I know what he means but I don't want to say it aloud. A chill sweeps down my spine.

Logan pulls up to a shiny-new stop sign on Semanski Street, and finally turns to look at me, anger burning in his eyes. "He slipped something in her drink."

"Oh God," I say.

He turns away and drives through the four-way stop. "So that kicked off part two of the fight. He was crouched down, putting his other shoe on and I flew at him in a rage, and it turned ugly. Really fast. It was bad, Harper. Really bad. It took half the football team to pull me off him. I told him I'd kill him."

My breathing turns shallow.

"You don't understand what it's like to be related to someone like that. To know that we share *anything*, let alone DNA. *Identical* DNA. If he would have gone through with that . . . with what he must have been planning . . . I would have murdered him. I'm not just saying that. He'd be a dead man if he had done it."

Despite myself I reach out and grasp his hand. Squeezing it to comfort the shattered guy sitting beside me.

"He didn't, Logan."

His voice cracks. "I know but I can't stand looking at him every day, knowing what he's capable of. I wanted to move here without him. I wanted to leave him back in Cedar Cove." Logan turns to me. "I promise you . . . I swear to you, I'll never let him touch you. Please, just don't let me lose you, too. I've lost so much because of him. I can't do it again."

I'm gutted, sitting here beside him, finally understanding everything he's been through, finally understanding why it was so important to him to keep me away from Daemon . . . from Trent.

I lean my forehead against the glass. "I'll give you tonight. And then, Logan, I don't know . . ."

CHAPTER TWENTY-FIVE

I slide out of Logan's car, holding my dress up off the ground. The rain darkens the cement parking lot as Logan rounds the car and grabs my hand.

"Are you ready for this, Madam President?" he asks, grinning. But there's something hesitant, timid about it, like he's afraid he's not allowed to smile right now.

"As ready as I'll ever be," I say.

We're only halfway to the building when the rain thickens, drenching my bare shoulders. Logan pulls my hand and we run across the curtain of rain, laughing as we make it to the overhang. The rain intensifies even further, pounding the roof until it's hard to make out the heavy bass beat coming from the gym doors.

"Do you hear that?" Logan asks.

"I can't hear anything," I say, laughing.

"It's either thunder or the DJ . . ." His voice trails off as it gets louder, and when he meets my eyes, there's something like fear in them. But then it's gone.

We walk to the gym, his dress shoes clacking on the cement. Allie and Adam should be here soon. It's too bad Bick didn't have anyone to go with. Maybe Allie and I should try to introduce him to some new girls. He hasn't dated since Madison ripped out his heart and stomped all over it.

We step in through the double doors, and the heavy beat of a hip-hop song greets us. Orange lights span back and forth from the rafters, and the walls are plastered with the butcher paper that Allie and a bunch of us decorated. As promised, papier-mâché spiders dangle down from the rafters.

The crowd is thick, decked out in fake blood and torn dresses, bloody gashes and green hair. Fog drifts among them, from where, I'm not sure.

"This is cool," Logan says. "We didn't have anything like it in Cedar Cove."

I stiffen at the thought of Cedar Cove, at the image that swarms my vision. A grainy, black-and-white picture of Trent Townsend.

But tonight isn't about Daemon, or Trent, or whatever I'm supposed to call him. It's about me and Logan.

The band switches to a slow song, and he turns to me. "Do you want to dance?"

I smile and look down, shy, and then back up at him. "Number three," I say, nodding toward the floor.

"You have a fear of dancing?"

"Dancing in public," I correct, blushing.

He pulls me against him. "This is one I can cure you of," he says, taking my hand.

I relish the familiar warmth as he leads me toward the dance floor, butterflies swarming like mad.

We push our way past ghouls and goblins, Frankensteins and undead cheerleaders. I do a double take when I pass a guy with a bloody slash on his neck, then blink away the image. It's fake, of course. I feel stupid for the way my heart jumped at the sight of him.

My shoes vibrate with the intensity of the bass as Logan pulls me into the center of the floor. "Put your arms around my shoulders," he says.

I lift my left arm, resting it on his shoulder, and then look down at my injured one. "I can't lift this arm above my chest," I say.

"It's okay. This will have to do," he says, sliding my right arm around his back. It's awkward and a little silly, but I don't resist.

He puts his arms around my back and pulls me against him, and I rest my head against his chest, breathing him in and willing my heart to calm. God I missed him. I had no idea how much I'd wrapped everything up in him until he was gone.

"Now, there's nothing to it. Just sway back and forth," he says.

I do as he instructs, though I feel awkward and out of place.

The song bleeds into another, and I slowly find the rhythm of it, allowing my body to relax into the beat.

All I can think is I'm glad I didn't miss this. It's stupid to want so desperately to be with Logan when I know I shouldn't be, but right now, it doesn't matter. Right now, we're together.

I stand more upright when the song ends, feeling a little light-headed with it all. "I'm going to go use the restroom. Meet me back here in five minutes?"

Logan nods.

I push my way through the thickening crowd. We've gotta be breaking a fire code or something with how many people are in the gym.

Finally, I emerge on the other side and walk down the hall, my flats quiet on the tiles. At the end of the long hall, I push into the bathroom, the door silent on its hinges.

I stop halfway to the stall, staring at the blotchy, mascara-covered face in the mirror. Madison. She freezes.

We eye each other across the small room, neither of us moving.

And then Madison breaks the spell and turns back to the mirror, trying to wipe the dark trails off her cheek. "I got stood up, if you must know."

I swallow. "I'm sorry."

She shrugs. "I put this stupid dance together, and I'm the one who gets dumped. Go figure."

A weird sense of triumph swirls in my gut. But as soon as I take another look at the bedraggled mess formerly known as Madison Vaughn, it's quickly dispelled by a stronger sense of pity. I reach over and pull a paper towel from the dispenser, getting it wet in the sink before I hand it to her. "Here."

She eyeballs it for a long moment, and then accepts it, dabbing away the dark tracks of mascara. I've never seen her looking less than perfect before. "Why are you being nice to me?" she asks.

I shake my head. "Not sure. Consider it a lapse in judgment."

She smiles softly through her tears. "Well, thanks, I guess."

"Yeah. Well, have a good one." I turn away and head back down the hall, eager to leave the twilight zone behind.

"Hey," she calls out. I stop in the door and turn to face her.

"Look, I know I'm a bitch to you," she says. "It's just, you have everything and you make it look so easy."

I narrow my eyes. "Is that supposed to be some kind of joke?"

She dabs at the last bit of mascara. Her eyes are still red, but the makeup looks better.

"I'm serious. You dress like a freaking farmer and guys like Logan still fall at your feet. And do you know how impressed Bick was when you signed up for that stupid welding class?"

I blink. "Oh," I say, surprised she knows I'm in ag mechanics. "I mean, it's not really like that."

"You can date whoever you want, and your friends don't care. They wouldn't harass you for days and days. They wouldn't mock the idea of you asking him to Tolo."

All at once, understanding dawns.

She's not talking about me anymore. She's talking about her and Bick.

"You dumped him because your friends weren't okay with it?"

"You have no idea what I do every day. How early I get up to get ready for school."

"I don't know what to say," I say, as the world, I'm sure, spins and tilts and rearranges itself. Is Madison actually being *honest* with me? Did she actually *like* Bick, and then dump him because her friends didn't approve?

Just then, the door swings open. A girl with red hair and a faux shredded dress—is she supposed to be a zombie?—walks in. She has too much makeup on to figure out who she is, but when she calls out, "Hey Madison!" I know they're friends.

Madison leans into me, lowering her voice. "Don't say anything. To anyone. Because if you do, you'll regret it. Got it?"

And *there's* the Madison I know and loathe. "Right. Sure."

I turn and shove the door back open, stepping into the hall. My head spins as I walk back to the gym, pondering the weird twist of events. How is it possible Madison is jealous of *me?*

"Why do you look so happy?"

I look up to see Allie standing just inside the double doors. She's wearing a white, fluffy miniskirt, a sleeveless white turtleneck, and enormous white wings.

"Wow. You guys are going as angels?"

She grins. "I'm an angel, Adam's the devil."

I chuckle. "Nice."

"Thanks, it was my idea," she says, spinning in a little pirouette. "You look gorgeous too. Great dress."

"Thanks." I look down, fluff out my Victorian-style gown. "Where is the Prince of Darkness?"

"Parking the car. It's pouring out there, so he dropped me off at the front," she says, jutting a thumb over her shoulder.

"Oh."

"Are you here with Logan?"

I nod.

"Do you think that's a good idea?" she asks, tipping her head to the side.

"We're at a school event. Nothing's going to happen. And as it turns out . . . he has a good reason for everything. I'll fill you in on it after the dance," I say, edging toward the gym doors. "I'm going to go find him."

"Okay. Catch up with you later?"

"Yeah. We should all do a late dinner or something."

"Sounds good." As I step away, she touches my arm. "Be safe, okay?

I swallow and nod, turning to push my way back into the gym, elbowing through the crowds, just as the song transitions to something upbeat. I see Logan's head bobbing above my classmates', so I squeeze my way through the crowd until I'm standing in front of him.

He doesn't even have to ask, just pulls me against him. We adjust to accommodate the uptempo, swaying and stepping more quickly. He holds me by the waist, his hips moving with mine. I laugh, because it feels a little awkward and oh-so-good at the same time.

I wrap my arms more tightly around him, pulling his body even closer against mine. Then I turn to his ear, whispering, "Number two."

He pulls back and stares into my eyes, waiting for the answer.

I lean forward, my lips touching his ear. "This one has

nothing to do with my mom and everything to do with my dad."

Logan raises a brow and waits for me, so I lean back in to shout into his ear. "I'm alone all the time, just waiting for someone like you to come along. I was afraid I'd fall for the wrong boy."

Logan stares down at me for a moment, the softest of smiles tugging at his lips, and then pulls me against him, and I feel the heat of him up and down my body. "That's one fear we don't need to worry about," he whispers into my ear.

He pulls back, tangling his fingers in my hair as he leans down to meet me, his lips crashing into mine.

Burning desire courses through my veins as he deepens the kiss and I slide my good arm up his shoulders, my hand gliding over his neck. My fingers burying themselves in his unruly dark hair.

When he tilts his head, my thumb slides further back, and as it pushes his hair aside, it meets bare skin.

I jerk. Bare skin, where it should be hair. We kiss again, and the thought dangles at the edge of my mind.

And then I freeze, horror sweeping over me. Just like that I'm standing in Logan's basement, watching the darkness swarm in Daemon's—Trent's—eyes as he readjusts his ball cap, giving me a glimpse of that jagged, angry scar behind his left temple.

I wrench away. For a moment, his hands just tighten over me, and I have to push him, hard. He stumbles back and we stand there, three feet apart. I stare at him with wild eyes as he looks back, confused.

"You're not Logan," I say.

His jaw drops, but he recovers quickly, stepping toward me. "Harper—"

"You have the same scar as Trent," I say, my voice shaking. Tears spring to my eyes. My chest heaves, and one thought echoes over the heavy bass beat of the song: I just kissed Trent.

I whirl around and run, shoving my way through the crowds, desperate to get away.

"*Hey!*" Someone yells as I elbow them hard. They glare at me with black eyes—contacts—but I just keep going. I have to get away from Daemon—Trent—whoever he is, have to find Adam. Someone I can trust.

Why did he tell me all that stuff in the car if he was Trent the whole time? Is this some kind of game to them? Am *I* some kind of game?

I don't even know what's true anymore, what's an elaborate lie. I'm swimming in too many of them.

The crowd is too thick near the front doors, and Trent's catching up with me. Where is Logan? How could Trent take his car and pick me up and not get caught?

I can't be near him. I don't want to talk to him, don't want him to touch me. I make a wide arc and find the back door, my heart beating out of control. I only saw Allie two, three minutes ago. Adam's probably still out there, parking the car.

If I can only just make it to him . . .

I shove my way outside, onto the covered walkway, and the upbeat song melts into the heavy hum of the pouring rain.

Lightning streaks across the sky, lighting up the lot like it's dawn.

I see Adam's Samurai at the far edge of the lot, near the tennis courts. I dash out into the rain, racing toward his car as the door to the gym flies open behind me.

"Harper, damn it!" Trent yells.

I run faster, my feet splashing through puddles, soaking through my shoes. The strands of my wig hang down around my face, dripping wet in an instant.

Trent's dress shoes pound on the concrete behind me, catching up. I make it to Adam's Samurai, yank on the handle.

But the door is locked and no one's in the car.

My heart slams into my throat and I whirl around. "Stay away from me!" I scream.

Trent skids to a stop, puts his hands up like he's trying to corner a wild animal.

"Harper, calm down," he says. His eyes are dark, shadowed behind the mask, and his hair is plastered to his face.

"I will not calm down! You are not my boyfriend!"

"Yes I am," he says, creeping forward. "Please, just calm down."

"Stop lying. I know you're not him."

"And how do you know that?"

"Because you have a scar," I say, backing into the Samurai. "The same scar as Trent."

He stops a few feet shy of me. "They're similar. They're not identical. I'm not him."

"It's in the same place," I say, now trembling. The rain has

235

soaked me to the bone, and my dress hangs around me, heavy with it. I yank off the wig and drop it to the wet concrete.

"We were both seriously injured in the accident. The car rolled, Harper."

I want to believe him, but I'm sick of trying so hard to trust him when nothing he says adds up.

"I don't believe you. Back up," I say. "Back up!" I yell. "I'm going back to the gym and you're going home. I'll get a ride with Adam and you're going home alone and that's going to be the end of us." I pause and shake my head. "The end of me and Logan. I don't even know who you are."

"Harper—"

"Back up!" I scream, the panic rising.

He blanches, hesitates. I'm about to run, and then it's too late.

He's on me in a second, slamming my head into Adam's car, and then the world goes black.

CHAPTER TWENTY-SIX

W hen I come to, my head pounds so hard I want to vomit.
My mouth tastes chalky and dry, like I spent the last
twenty minutes eating cotton balls. I'm laying on something
hard and cold, my cheek smashed down.

I sit up on my elbows and blink against the haze, everything
coming into focus.

I'm in an empty room. The lights are off, save one in the
hall with an ornate, stained glass cover that splashes a rain-
bow of muted light across the aged hardwood floors. I twist
around. The window behind me is open, strong wind whipping through the gap.

I turn back and stare at the glass fixture for a long time,
and then down at the old hardwood floors beneath my feet.
Blinking, I finally realize where I am—an empty room on the
second floor of Logan's house.

Lightning flashes, and I jerk back as I see him—Trent,
leaning against the wall in the corner. I stifle my scream,

and he smiles back at me, his white teeth flashing in the darkness.

My collarbone pounds, waves of pain washing over me. He put me down so I'm lying right on it, and it feels worse than the day it broke.

"So glad you could finally join me. I thought maybe I'd been too rough with your head."

"Logan's going to kill you for this," I say.

His grin grows wider. "Ahh, see, I thought you really *had* figured it out. But you haven't yet, have you?"

I swallow, nerves intensifying. What haven't I figured out? What else is he hiding? I sit all the way up, cradling my arm. Why had I ditched the brace and sling in favor of the pretty dress? I can barely think through the blinding pain.

"Logan!" I scream, desperate. He has to be in the house. He has to help me.

What if he's not? What if Trent did something to him?

"*Logan!*" he yells, imitating me. Then he laughs.

Fear creeps up my spine. The way he says it brings a moment of clarity. "His name's not Logan, is it?"

He shakes his head, his lips pursed as if he's fighting a smile, but he's doing a poor job of masking his pleasure. He likes that I don't have it all figured out, likes that he's holding the strings.

"Why are you looking at me like that?" I ask.

"Ask me. Ask me what his name is."

I swallow. "What's his name?"

And now the grin is wide, ear-to-ear. "Trent."

Ice grips my veins, turns my insides out. "You're lying. You're Trent. I saw the articles. I know what you did."

"Do I really have to spell it out? Look around, Harper. Does this look like a bedroom to you?" He stares at me, that same proud smile on his face.

I look around the empty room. Look at the bare hardwoods, the blank walls. This is supposed to be Logan's room.

But it's empty.

Horror washes over me, and like the last piece of a puzzle, this empty room snaps into place, and in an instant, I see the whole picture, and I know.

I know why Logan didn't tell me about his brother at first. I know why he hid everything from me, why he lied over and over and over. I know why the boy at the dance—the boy who held me close and so right—has the same scar as the boy in the basement.

I know why Logan never wanted me to sit down with him and Daemon.

He didn't want to because he couldn't.

There is no twin brother.

I think I might be sick. I think I may vomit right there. "But I saw the pictures of you two."

He laughs. "Don't look so nauseated," he says, his voice cool, calm, collected. "See there *were* two of us. Once. Trent— who you know as Logan—he just loves to cart those pictures around. No one ever questions why we don't have any recent ones of us together."

"Your mother's accident."

I'd assumed the pictures stopped because the happy times died with his mother. Not because one of them died too.

He nods. "Yes. We were in the car *together* when dear old Mom careened off the road. I was behind her. The driver's side took the brunt of the damage. And stupid, spoiled Trent was in the front passenger seat."

I blink, stare. So there were two of them . . . and now there's one? But if Trent lived through the accident and Daemon died, why is he the one standing in front of me?

My head is spinning so hard I can barely process it.

"See, Harper, some souls just don't want to let go. I was supposed to die; he was supposed to live. But I couldn't quite handle that. Call it unfinished business. Call it revenge. Trent got everything he ever wanted. He had all the friends, the girls, the sports trophies, even my dad. And he was the one who got to stick around while I was supposed to die? Wasn't going to happen."

Behind me, the rain intensifies, pounding against the window as another bolt of lightning flashes across the sky, making dark shadows on his face. "So I hung around for a while, biding my time. Call me a ghost, a soul, whatever. But I had unfinished business, and I wasn't going to let it go. Then when Trent was under the knife so the doctors could repair his injuries from the accident, I took my opportunity and just . . . slipped in. He never liked sharing things with me. Rather poetic that I forced him to share a body, eh?"

I grind my teeth. "That's not possible."

"Oh really? And you would know . . . how?"

"Because it's ridiculous!" I say, my voice rising, hysterical.

I hold my arm tightly against my body as I climb to my feet. Blood rushes to my head and my temple pounds harder. "A person can't just die and take over someone else's body! He's still here, and his name isn't Daemon or Trent. It's Logan."

Daemon twists his head at a funny angle, his glare slicing through me. "Now you're pissing me off, Harper. And you don't want to do that."

"Please—"

"Shut up," he snaps. "The Logan you know doesn't exist. And Trent is . . . let's call it taking a nap."

I nod. I'll do anything to pacify him, calm him down. "Daemon, I'm sorry—"

"How badly do you think he wants to keep you? He can never just tell the truth, can he? He's so desperate to cover me up he'd do anything. He doesn't want anyone to know his brother is still here. He always did think he was better than me." He pauses for a second, his eyes sweeping over me. "He probably likes you, even. Never did have good taste in girls."

He purses his lips, then shakes his head. "Some of those stories he made up just to keep you . . . ridiculous. Then again, you bought it, didn't you? Today's story, on the way to the masquerade, before I took over? Bravo. Academy Award winning speech, really."

I glance around, trying to figure out the best escape route. There are only two: the window—across the roof, and down the round columns to the ground—or the bedroom door. "So you can . . . see us? Even when . . ." I swallow. "Even when he's the one in control?"

241

Daemon beams at me. "Yep. I don't think he's figured that one out yet. He has no *idea* what I do, I can tell. But I always was the stronger one. It's frustrating when I can't totally control him, but at least I can watch."

I glimpse hopelessly at the window. We're on the second floor. I can't escape over the roof either.

Daemon slips something out of his pocket, and I realize with horror it's the rusty hook from the basement. He twists it in his hands, and the panic doubles. If I scream, would anyone hear me? I need him to keep talking. Need him to turn back into Logan somehow. If that's really how it works . . .

"This town is too small," he says, surprising me.

"Huh?"

"There's not a lot of things to do, havoc to wreak."

It dawns on me, what he's saying. "You did more than the stop signs and the car accident."

He nods.

"The bloody cow bones?"

He grins. "Genius, right?"

"The birds?"

He nods. My breathing turns shallow.

"Bick's quad?

He scowls. "See, that one was meant for him. Didn't expect you to be the one on it, so I had to go back and wreck his truck just to get him. Guess it all worked out, though. That collarbone must hurt like a bitch." He lights up. "Would have been better had you died, but I suppose that's asking too much."

He looks past me, out the window.

"What do you have against Bick?"

"He likes you."

I blink. Huh?

"See, it's like the world playing out on a big screen, except I'm seeing it through Trent's eyes. And I saw you two that day in the parking lot. Saw Bick spring to your rescue, try to go knight in shining armor and get the blood off your window."

He slides a finger over the hook, playing with the point of it. "But you couldn't get together with Bick. I needed you to be with Trent. He's always been such a stupid sucker for love. If Bick got in the way of that, I'd have less to use against Trent." Daemon shrugs. "It was Trent who cleaned your window, you know. I think he knew it was me. He didn't realize you'd already seen the handprint."

"How'd you do it? How'd you get the handprints on the windows in the middle of the day? Logan—" I gulp, catching myself. "Trent must have been in charge of your . . ." My voice trails off. "Your body. I had class with him. Ate lunch with him. He was totally normal."

"Fifty bucks and a couple of freshman," he says, laughing. "Shockingly simple, I know. Trent was a little confused by that one. I usually take care of things on my own."

Lightning crashes outside, and I look out at the branches of the trees whipping together in the wind. Why does Logan— Trent—have to live so far away from everything? If I get out of this house somehow, do I even stand a chance? "Why'd you bring me here?"

Daemon shrugs. "Because I can't *physically* hurt Trent, but destroying you would kill him. One of these days, he's going to join me on the dark side. If he would just stop fighting me, I think we could figure out a way to share this body, but he's not convinced. He keeps trying to walk a tight line, play by society's rules, when I'd like to do anything but." He lights up, staring down at me with a look of such perverse pleasure, I want to shrink into myself. "The less he has to live for, the less he's going to fight me for dominance. How much of his life do I have to ruin before he gives in?"

I glance back at the window again, then turn to Daemon. The window will never work. I have to get past him, somehow, and down the stairs. The only way it will work is if I catch him off guard.

"Do you remember when he told you how our dad died?" he asks, stepping toward me. I scoot back on the floor.

"A heart attack," I say, nodding.

Daemon's bark of laughter is so abrupt I jump. "See, dear old dad was *poisoned*. Same stuff I used on the birds, actually. A little harder to get my hands on oleander up here, but I managed."

I can't breathe as the room seems to close in, pressure building in my chest. If he's willing to kill his own father, he won't mind killing me.

"Lucky for me, I had no motive for killing dad . . . or at least no motive those dumb cops could figure out." He grins.

"They'll find out eventually," I volunteer, but my words are hollow and even I don't believe them.

"Hah!" Daemon cackles. "Not likely. And let's not forget about mommy dearest," he says.

My throat burns with unshed tears. "He said it was a car accident," I choke out. "A deer ran out."

He shakes his head, tsks. "He's right about the accident. But she swerved because I told her what I'd done to Dad. Just to see the expression on her stupid face. She favored Trent too, you know. Hid it better than Dad, but I could see it. I just didn't count on her reacting like that. She just completely blanked out, didn't even attempt to turn at the next curve."

Tears glimmer in my eyes, make it hard to see him. There's gotta be some way to get Logan—Trent back. If I say something, do just the right thing . . .

"Just tell me what you want from me," I say. "I'll do anything."

"Me? I want nothing from you. But Trent wants you, which makes you rather useful to me. He gets everything he wants and blames all the bad stuff on me. I was never good enough for him . . . for *anyone* when I was alive, and I'm not good enough when we share a body."

When he runs his hand through his still rain-dampened hair, I get the barest glimpse of his scar, hidden in the thick, wavy strands. How could I have spent so much time with Logan and never seen it?

"I get to punish Trent every day for the rest of my life. Either he gives in and we share this body fair and square, or I ruin everything he has."

He stares straight at me with that intense smile of his, and my heart lodges in my throat. "Your time is nearly up, Harper."

But it's not. It can't be. I scramble to my feet and lunge past him, tearing through the doorway and into the hallway. I scramble down the stairs so fast I trip over my own feet, grabbing at the banister to save myself. But as I yank myself to a stop, my body swings around and my shoulder slams into the wall. Tears, instant, well in my eyes as my breath disappears.

I turn back to the stairs and rush down the last few, to the first landing, but he's on me, grabbing my hair and yanking me back. I elbow him hard in the gut, and he grunts, releasing me as he stumbles down a few steps and doubles over. "You bitch," he grinds out.

He's blocking the stairs. When he stands again, anger blazing in his eyes, I whirl around and race back up the steps. I hit the top step, skidding on an area rug, barely saving myself.

I cross the empty bedroom, putting my foot through the windowsill just as he darkens the doorway. My dress rides up as I duck under the windowpane.

I'm only halfway out when he grabs my ankle, yanking hard. I scream and pull away, desperate. I lean back and kick violently, and my toe catches him on the chin. He curses and lets me go, and I tumble onto the roof.

My heart, already scrambling, turns into a thunderous roar as I skid on a leaf, tumbling down the slope of the rain-slickened, moss-covered rooftop. There's no way to stop myself. I scramble, grabbing at anything in sight as I roll toward the edge, catching myself on an attic vent near the gutters, but it's not enough to stop my body's movement. My legs swing out over the edge and dangle toward the ground as rain slides past me, pours over the edge of the rotten soffits. The darkened clouds make it hard to see into the light blazing from his bedroom window.

I blink, trying to see through the raindrops, searching the roofline for his shadow.

"You're gonna regret that," he says, spitting the words as he steps into view, looming high above me. I must have split his lip, because blood trickles down his chin, making him look all the more sinister. He's on the roof above me, stepping slowly down toward the gutter. The muscles in my left arm tremble as my grip slides, until I'm hanging on with scarcely more than a fingertip.

I wonder if this is how my mom felt before she died. If she hung on desperately, hoping someone would come in time to save her. If she knew, as her fingers slid, that she was about to die.

I glance over my shoulder. There are no shrubs here, just too-long grass at least a dozen feet below. He takes another step toward me as the lightning flashes, and then my fingers slip, and I'm falling.

I land, hard, on the dampened, muddy earth below, the wind slamming from my lungs. I lie there, my mouth open like a fish gasping for air, the rain blinding me.

I'm alive.

I'm really alive.

When I finally regain my breath, I wipe my eyes free of the rain and look up at the roof, expecting to see Daemon staring down at me.

But he's not there. I blink, searching the darkness for his face, but he's gone. I climb to my feet, still cradling my arm and gasping for air as I tear across the lawn and into the dark shadows of the woods, just as the door to the house slams open.

I'm not far into the tree line before I realize I'm no match for him. He's crashing through the brush with the speed of a raging bull. My foot slips in the mud and I go down, slamming to the ground just as I hear his strange laughter behind me.

My fingers touch something soft, hidden in the fallen leaves.

Heart hammering out of control, I push the leaves aside, and a scream dies in my throat. I cover my mouth with my hands and stare, gagging.

Two glassy, lifeless eyes stare back at me, deeply sunken, emotionless. His face is pale, waxy.

Dead.

It's his uncle, half-buried in the dampened earth under a big cedar tree.

He killed his uncle.

This whole time, he wasn't away on business, he was dead and rotting. The horror building in my chest, threatening to suffocate me, nearly makes me break down in sobs, but I can't. There's no time.

I climb to my feet, nausea swelling as I take off again, desperate, frantic for a savior, a safety net, something.

Anything.

The rain drips down my face, into my eyes, making it hard

to see where I'm going. I leap over a tree root, the panic overwhelming me. My shoulder is numb now, completely devoid of pain.

He's getting closer with every second. He curses as a tree branch snaps, and I realize he's closing in on me. I push faster, my feet slipping as the rain deafens the sound of my muddy footsteps.

I'll never make it to the road, to another house. He lives so far away from anything. I have to hide or outsmart him or . . .

Or he'll kill me.

Lightning cracks across the sky, for the first time in many minutes, and then the thunder rumbles, slow and quiet at first, and then building until it drowns out everything else. I force my screaming muscles to move faster and faster as I careen through the trees like a bat out of hell.

Too late, I realize what I've done. Ahead and below, the Green River rages. There's a cliff. It must be two hundred feet tall, towering over the valley.

A beautiful vantage point for him to catch up, corner me.

Shit. Shit shit shit.

I skid to a stop, whirl around, rethink my plan. There's gotta be something. Some way out of here, somewhere to hide.

I turn again and peer over the ledge, and that's when I see it. A thin, tiny trail leading down to a series of rock ledges. I could climb down there. Hide. The trail is almost completely concealed.

But the idea of climbing down sends panic streaking up and

down my limbs, and all I picture is my mom tumbling to her death.

It occurs to me then that Logan never discovered my number one fear: falling. Just like my mom.

I'm still staring down when I hear Daemon's voice drifting through the brush, cursing as he thrashes through.

I have no other choice. I slip behind the fern, edging down the path, my toes perilously close to the ledge. It's skinny, maybe eighteen inches wide. I have to step sideways, my back sliding along the rocks, as I make it to the first landing.

I can't hear anything now, save the rain pounding the ground all around me, and I wait only a moment to heave a deep breath before following the next part of the trail. My left foot—the foot I lead with—slides slightly on the trail, and with a gasp, I look down.

Trees and rocks and the river, all so far away the trees look more like sticks. I would die if I fell down there. I would die, just like my mother.

I tear my gaze away and look back at the path, concentrating on sliding one foot and then the other, scooting to the narrow rock ledge.

And then the trail widens and I'm there, on the final landing.

I collapse onto the ground.

I did it.

I really did it.

For a moment, I think, *Logan is going to be so proud of me.* But then reality hits—there is no Logan, not really. I curl up, sliding back against the rock, trying to make myself invisible.

Then I close my eyes as I listen for Daemon, praying he didn't see me come down here. If he finds me, it's all over. I'm dead. There's nowhere to go from here.

The rain is streaming down the cliffside, forming a tiny river as it pools around me. I shiver, curling tighter, and then I hear it. The sound of clothing brushing along the cliffside. I snap my eyes open and see Daemon edging toward me.

Shit. I scramble to my feet and look around, but there are no more trails, nothing but a ten-foot-wide landing a dozen feet below, and then two hundred feet more to the flooding river.

Daemon steps onto the landing just a half-dozen feet way from me, smiling, his hair plastered to his face and his eyes dark. He's lost his mask somewhere. Tears swim in my vision, mingling with the raindrops sliding down my skin. It can't be this way.

It can't end like this.

CHAPTER TWENTY-SEVEN

A sole bolt of lightning streaks across the sky, the second since I ran from the house. It makes odd shadows in the cliff side, its light filtering through what branches hang over the edge from the trees towering above us. It turns his face into harsh angles.

And then it dawns on me. "It's the lightning," I say through the tears burning in my throat.

"Huh?"

"Logan . . . Trent told me it was storming when you went off the road with your mother. The lightning must trigger your switch. Every time I've seen you . . ."

I think back to the day he scared me in the basement, the day I followed him down the darkened roads.

It was storming.

Maybe that means if I can keep him calm, keep him from doing anything drastic, until the storm lets up, Logan . . . Trent will come back. I think. I don't know. Maybe it doesn't work that way. But the storm has been lessening. The end of it has to be near.

I swallow. "The lightning triggers your . . ." I repeat, "your switch."

"It started that way," he says, grinning. "It had to be a full lightning storm for him to be so lost in memories I could slip in, take over. But I'd get so weak from being in control, he'd come back just as soon as the storm ended. But I'm getting better. Sometimes I can last a whole day in control or even take control when a storm is far off in the distance. It's harder, but I can do it."

His voice has such a note of pride in it I think I might be sick. "It was me up at Evan's Creek, you know. That was the first time I controlled him without a full thunderstorm right in our area. Pity it didn't last longer. You just *had* to go and smack my arm. It was just enough to break my concentration, and Trent regained control."

Horror washes over me. I step back, closer to the edge of the ravine. Far below me, the Green River rages, frothy and cold. If it's even possible to survive a fall this far, I'd die from the river. I need to stall. Just keep him talking until the storm is over.

"Tell me what really happened in Cedar Cove. Don't I deserve to know?"

"You're going to die, and *that's* your final wish? To know what I did six months ago?" He laughs. "Hell, I'll give you this one. Rather nice story, I think, much better than what Trent made up. But the story about *you* will top it."

I wince and fight the urge to step back again, to where the ground is unstable, held together with the strength of tree roots and ferns.

"See, there was this girl who thought she was too good for me. I asked her out, before my mom's accident. She turned me down, but a month later, she's hooking up with Trent. We're fucking twins, and she still chooses him over me.

"Fast forward a few months, and I'm stuck in his body. Logan went to prom with her, and they took a limo. See, this was when I still needed the lightning to trigger my switch. It started storming, and I guess he had no way of getting home before I took over." He grins widely, his white teeth flashing in the darkness reminding me of a wolf. "Of course, I couldn't disappoint her, so I went to the after-party. Decided I'd have my fun with her, but I got caught, and things got ugly. A football player thought he'd defend her virtue or some bullshit."

He laughs. "Turns out football players aren't good fighters. Even two on one, I had the upper hand. Course, there was a whole team to back them up. Nearly got us locked up for that one, but they couldn't prove I'd drugged her, and the other guy swung first. So I lay low for a bit, let Trent handle things while the dust settled."

"And you moved here."

"Yep. And then 'Logan,'" Daemon says, making quotes, "meets you, and you fall for him, and the two of you go to a dance. Are you sensing a trend yet?" He steps forward, so only a dozen feet separate us. I glance around, desperate for some kind of answer, for some way to get out of this.

254

"Why'd you kill your uncle?"

"He caught me with the stop signs. He got in the way of what I was doing," Daemon says. "My only regret is not being able to see Trent's face when he realized what I'd done. Should have written it on a mirror, or something, so I could witness it. Man, that musta been pretty spectacular."

My chest aches for Logan . . . for Trent. For everything he's done to try to live a normal life.

Daemon sighs, this happy, drawn-out sigh that makes my skin crawl. My stomach spasms and I think I might lose my lunch. This is it. This is what it comes down to.

Another bolt of lightning. I count in my head, *One Mississippi, two Mississippi . . .* I'm all the way to eight before the thunder arrives. It's almost over. Logan might come back. I might live through this.

But a dark look passes over Daemon's features. He lowers his body a bit, and for a second I think he's going to crouch.

But he's not.

He's pushing off, racing at me. He's going to throw me off the cliff.

My pulse thunders in my ears, and I do the only thing I can think of. I drop to my knees, curl over.

His shins slam into me, and I grab the dripping fern near my hands as Daemon's body flies over me, over the cliff.

Just a second later, I hear a sickening thump. I crawl to the edge of the cliff and look down.

Ten feet below me, his body sits, twisted on a hard rock ledge, one leg dangling down toward the hundred-plus-foot drop. A trickle of blood drips down the rock, into the dark abyss below.

I sit back and slump into the ground, the relief and sorrow so swift I feel like a puddle on the ground.

It's over.

It's really over.

EPILOGUE

Six months later . . .

I'm sitting on a bench near the student library, a novel in my hands, but I can't seem to concentrate. I've been staring at the same page for five minutes.

He should be here by now. I wonder what's keeping him.

I turn the page, but it's useless because I don't remember the last page I read, or the page before that, or the page before that.

I sigh, snap it shut, and look out across the courtyard, blinking away the glare from the bright white pages in the sunshine.

My cell rings, and I recognize the personalized ring tone. Smiling, I flip it open.

"Hey Dad," I say.

"Hey," he says. "So I'm at the grocery store, and I can't remember what kind of sauce you said he likes."

In the background, an overhead speaker comes to life. I wait for it to finish, chuckling under my breath. My dad attempting to cook dinner for us is amusing on so many levels. "Bolognese."

He says something under his breath, but I can't make it out. "They make that in jars, right?"

"Yeah. It should be with the other sauces."

"Okay. See you when you get home."

"Great. Love you," I say.

"Love you too."

I snap my phone shut, slipping it back into my pocket. It's the third time this week my dad has called my cell. Six months ago I would have bet money he didn't even have my number programmed into his phone. But when he nearly lost me that rainy night . . .

Things changed. He finally got the wake-up call he needed.

I shove my discarded book into my backpack and then pull my binder out, flipping to the last divider where a vinyl pouch can be found. I unzip the pouch and pull out a handful of printouts.

Logan's—no, Trent's—face stares back at me, along with a headline: LOCAL GIRL ESCAPES ATTEMPTED MURDER BY BOYFRIEND.

Another headline to go with the others that will come up if you Google Trent Townsend.

Even though I now know his real name is Trent, I still think of him as Logan. It's Logan I fell in love with. Logan I miss. Trent is a stranger.

"Hey DQ," a voice calls, and I look up.

"Hey yourself." I stand up, throw my backpack over my shoulder, and grin up at Bick.

"You ready to go? Cows wait for no man," he says.

"You're such a dork," I say, adjusting the straps of my backpack. My collarbone finally healed, though there's still a tiny bump.

"Beggars can't be choosers."

"Am I a beggar?"

He bumps my hip with his. "Hey, you wanted help for your dad, and I come cheap."

"Hey, he's making you dinner. And besides, I pay you in tutoring," I say.

"True, but are your services any good?"

I drop my jaw, indignant. "You got a B on your last chem test!"

"Fine, fine. I agree. You're worth the effort."

"Wow, I'm so flattered," I joke, fluttering a hand over my heart.

Bick looks down at me as we walk off campus, heading to his giant truck. It was fixable after all, though it took half of the ag mechanics crew and a whole lot of hammers and parts.

I don't know what this is, between us. He started helping a lot at my house, after my collarbone broke and Daemon nearly killed me. Just showed up one day with Adam and did my chores.

But even after Adam went back to business as usual, Bick kept coming around. And then . . . I started to feel something,

something that terrified me. It's nothing like the swept-away feeling I had with Logan. It's this achingly slow build, as the two of us edge closer and closer to a place I'm afraid to go, but unable to resist.

I know that, unlike Logan, it's okay to trust Bick, this guy I've known so many years, this guy who would do anything for me if only I ask.

Sometimes being strong isn't about keeping people away. Sometimes it's about letting them in.

"So if I pick up an extra milking on Saturday," he says, "what do I earn for *that*?"

I roll my eyes. "The pleasure of my company?"

"You're gonna hang out in the milk parlor for four hours with me?"

"Maybe. Maybe I'll even help," I say.

"Good. I might let you."

We're at his truck now, and we stop next to the passenger door. Bick puts his hand on the handle, but he doesn't open it right away. "Are you going to go visit him soon?"

I rest my hand on the truck to steady myself. I knew he'd ask, eventually. I just don't know the answer. "I'm not sure."

"I'll go with you, if you want. It's a long drive. Lots of freeway miles."

"Thanks," I say quietly, grateful that he understands, that I don't even have to ask him to go with me.

I guess the big irony of my list of fears was that the biggest one was never on my list: I was afraid to talk about them, let anyone help with them. Things with Logan went so horribly wrong, but I'd been willing to ignore it for so long because of what he was doing for me. How he was helping me get over the things that scared me.

But I never should have put that on his shoulders. I should have trusted my friends, too.

In the months since Logan's been locked away, Allie's taken me to swimming lessons and Bick's helped me learn to change lanes and merge on the freeway. Adam even took me four-by-fouring again, though he agreed to stick to the easy trails until I grew more confident.

Bick pulls open the passenger door, staring down at me. "Have you talked to him lately?"

I let my eyes lose focus, tracing over the small bump in my collarbone. The doctor says I'll always have it. He called it a badge of honor.

It'll always remind me of Logan. Of my first real boyfriend.

He's locked up about two hours north of here. Not in prison. His cell has padded walls. They don't believe that his brother's soul is fighting for dominance, they just think he's crazy. That he has multiple personality disorder or something.

But I saw it for myself. I know what really happened that night.

He writes to me, sometimes, says Daemon hasn't come back since he fell over the edge of the cliff. He thinks because his heart stopped for a few minutes in the ambulance, that Daemon finally died for good.

I don't know if I believe him. I hope it's true for his sake.

I blink away my thoughts, stop tracing over my collarbone

and meet Bick's eyes with a small smile. "No, I haven't seen him. I'd like to go, though. Soon."

"Sure. We can do that." Bick waits while I slide in, then pushes the door shut behind me. I'm surprised every time he does something sweet like that. He was always so rough around the edges.

But I guess even Madison saw past his exterior. And maybe she hurt him, but I see her, sometimes, watching us together, and I know she's jealous. I know she misses him. She has a good reason to.

He slams the door behind me and walks around to his side. He starts the truck up, and the big block engine he installed rumbles the floorboards. Before shifting into gear, he studies me. "Do you have to sit so far away?"

I look at him and feel a blush spread across my cheeks. And then I slide over so that our knees are touching.

"That's better."

And then he shifts his truck and leaves the school grounds behind.

ACKNOWLEDGMENTS

I owe a huge debt to Gillian for finding the heart of the story and guiding me to it. Your insight and attention to detail amaze me. Many thanks, too, to Jocelyn and the whole crew at Razorbill.

Thank you, Zoe, for spending a day spinning ideas with me when I had none. *Dangerous Boy* is the result of those e-mails, and it wouldn't exist if it weren't for you. And thank you, Nancy, for your help on covers and deadlines.

My gratitude to Dave and Brooke for your patience and love even when I'm knee-deep in edits.

Lastly, thank you to my readers, because without you, none of this would matter.